TEXAS TALES
YOUR TEACHER
NEVER TOLD YOU

C. F. Eckhardt

Republic of Texas Press

Library of Congress Cataloging-in-Publication Data

Eckhardt, Charles F.
    Texas tales your teacher never told you / Charles F. Eckhardt.
        p.   cm.
    ISBN 1-55622-141-X
    1. Tales—Texas.   2. Legends—Texas.
3. Texas—History—Republic, 1836-1846.   I. Title.
GR110.T5E25   1991
398.22'09764—dc20   91-17179
                                                          CIP

ISBN 1-55622-141-X
10 9 8 7 6 5
9106

All inquiries for volume purchases of this book should be addressed to
Wordware Publishing, Inc., at the above address. Telephone inquiries
may be made by calling:

(972) 423-0090

This book is dedicated to four people.

To my mother, Evelyn Hooper Eckhardt (1914-1986), who first recognized and encouraged my interest in the history and legends of Texas, and who recognized and promoted, in her quiet way, my urge to write.

To my wife, Vicki Jean Zeff Walker Eckhardt, who has endured some thirty years of the writer's struggle and has not as yet divorced or killed me, a fact which places her in the patience-league with a feller named Job.

To my daughter, Kristin Elaine Eckhardt Mueller, who listened to and liked her old Dad's stories when she was little.

And to my grandson, Stephen Clint Mueller, who has the good or ill fortune to have been nicknamed MacDuff at birth because he chanced to be grandson to a man who loves Shakespeare and he was delivered by Caesarian section—and who, with his contemporaries and those who follow, will have to find those Texas tales the teachers never tell somewhere outside a classroom.

Contents

THE HOW-COME OF THIS BOOK

As a general rule, our school courses in Texas history start about the time the Spaniards first came into Mexico and—except for a very brief few words on the end of the Republic and annexation—pretty well end about 4:48 P.M. on April 21, 1836, at San Jacinto. When I was a youngster, anything else you wanted to know about Texas history you got from J. Frank Dobie—or Zane Grey and Max Brand, if that's the direction your reading tastes ran—or from Gene Autry and Tex Ritter movies.

When we studied Texas history in school— and even if we pored over books like *Texas History Movies* in detail—we somehow got the impression that Sam Houston's Texas Army caught Santa Anna's men with their britches down at San Jacinto and proceeded to whip their drawers and socks off. Then the needle playing the time-record seemed to skip a couple of grooves and the next scene we saw was Dr. Anson Jones, last president of the Republic, hauling down the Lone Star at the log-house capitol in Austin so the Stars and Stripes could be run up. What we generally got was a statement that ran "Texas was a republic for ten years; Sam Houston, Mirabeau B. Lamar, David G. Burnet, and Anson Jones were the presidents; Stephen F. Austin died, the Republic of Texas went broke, it was annexed by the United States in 1846, and that led to war with Mexico in 1847."

That's what happened, all right—but that's by no means all that happened in those ten years. Texas declared its independence from Mexico at Washington-on-the-Brazos on March 2, 1836, won it at San Jacinto on April 21, 1836, and became a state of the United States at Austin on February 19, 1846. There's a lot of rip-roaring, blood-and-thunder history crammed into that twelve-days-less-than-ten-years, and—except for the studies and writings of those historians who specialize in "The Republic Period"—most of it gets pretty short shrift. Anything that happened after that usually gets pretty short shrift, too.

Me, I was a little different. I listened to tales told by old-timers. Some of 'em had been Indian fighters, some had been Rangers, some may have been fellers who heard the owl hoot, and some of 'em were just folks. A good many of 'em, in that fine old Texas phrase, had "done seed the elephant."

Some of these tales I heard across campfires. Some of 'em I heard in bars. Some of 'em I heard sitting around in backyards at night. Some of 'em I heard when I was a little feller, and some of 'em I heard later. Some of 'em have historical backing, some of 'em don't but are probably as true as anything that does, and some are just good stories. When a tale can be checked historically, I do that. I'm often able to flesh out a bare-bones tale with enough historical fact to make it worth telling. When a tale can't be checked out historically, I tell it like I heard it.

Some of these tales can be told to your children or grandchildren—even the very young ones. Some of 'em have enough blood and guts in 'em to give those kids, the ones who think slice 'n dice movies are the thing to see, nightmares they didn't figure on. Some of 'em get a mite spicy for the younger set. They're all tales of Texas—tales your teachers didn't tell you, but tales that shouldn't be allowed to die.

Most of these tales have appeared, in one form or another, in an historical newspaper column called *Charley Eckhardt's Texas*, which is dedicated to telling the old tales of Texas. Some of 'em have appeared in *The National Tombstone Epitaph*, which calls itself "The National Newspaper Of The Old West" and is published by the same firm and in the same place as the original *Tombstone Epitaph* that reported the O. K. Corral fight. Some of 'em have appeared, in slightly different forms, in other magazines in the United States and overseas. Some of 'em have never appeared anywhere but in this book.

There is, at the back of this book, a bibliography. You'll find in it the historical support for some of these stories. For others, you'll find no historical support at all. If you were to come up to me and put your trigger finger against my nose and say, "Eckhardt, where did you get such-and-such a statement in thus-and-so story?" I probably couldn't tell you right off. I might not be able to tell you at all—but I got it somewhere, sometime, from a source I considered accurate at the time.

This book is not "history." It is Texas Tales. It should be read as such. It was Texas Tales like these that made me—and a lot of other folks—get serious about studying history. If you like Texas Tales, here they are—enjoy 'em. If you don't—well, then, you ain't nothin' but a damYankee an' I don't give a damn what you think.

C. F. Eckhardt
Seguin, Texas

THE FIRST
ENGLISH-SPEAKER IN TEXAS

Who was the very first English-speaker to set foot in Texas?

Before I try to answer that question, let me ask another—who was the first non-Amerindian to set foot in Texas?

Let me try to answer the second question first. There exists, in China, what may be and probably is the oldest nonreligious book on the face of the earth. It is, in fact, some 500 years older than the first known written versions of the Jewish texts that became the basis for the Old Testament in our Bible. It was first compiled as a book—so a group of collected writings in a single place may be called before there were any books as we'd know them— about 3500 years ago, from accounts that may have been as much as 2000 years old when the collection was first compiled. It is called the Sun-Hai Ching or the Shun-Hai King, depending on how you choose to pronounce the archaic Chinese ideograms that serve as its title. The ideograms translate, roughly, to *Classic Of Mountains And Seas.*

The book contains accounts of explorations of lands known and unknown. One of those accounts is of an overland trek by a group of explorers whose names and nationality are unknown. Remember please, the collection is at least 3500 years old. The accounts may be as much as 5500 or even 6000 years old. The particular account I'm referring to seems to be one of the very oldest in the book.

This account describes, in great detail, an overland trek of about 1000 modern miles (as converted from Chinese li). The route of march has been computer-matched to virtually every possible stretch of land on the globe. It matches in all particulars only one—a strip of land ranging from 10 to 20 miles wide, beginning in central Wyoming and ending at the mouth of Santa Elena Canyon, in what is today Texas' Big Bend National Park.

The explorers, whomever they may have been, gave us descriptions of topography, minerals, and waterflow which match the Wyoming-to-Texas route, but they also described plants and animals. One of the animals they described was small and piglike, yet not a pig. The description fits the peccary, which is not a true pig but is the only pig-related beast native to the Americas. What's more, the explorers said their pig-like beast had a distinct collar of gray fur around its neck. That makes it Pecari Tajacu—the collared peccary or javelina—which is native only to the American Southwest and Mexico.

If these guys saw peccaries, they saw them in the Americas, because that's the only place there are or ever have been any peccaries. If they saw the collared peccary in particular, they saw him in West Texas, southern New Mexico, southern Arizona, or northern Mexico, because that's the only place the diminutive porker has ever lived.

Now, precisely how old is this account? No one knows for sure—not even the Chinese. We do know that China carried on an extensive trade with a place it called Fusang, where the people "barked like dogs," which is a fair approximation of what Athabascan—the Apache tongue—sounds like the first time you hear it. That trade was carried on for three to five hundred years and ended only about 1000 AD. This account had been in the Sun-Hai Ching for 2500 years before that.

We have a clue, though. Botanists tell us that the vegetable pepper—the pepper pod or "chili pepper"—and the legume we call the "peanut" are native to the Americas and to no other place on earth. Both pepper pods and peanuts have been, by written record, standard ingredients in Chinese cuisine for at least 2000 years. Pepper pod seeds and peanuts identical to primitive varieties still being grown in Mexico have been found by archaeologists, sealed in Chinese tombs which have not been disturbed for as long as 4000 years.

Now—who was the very first person, whose native language was English, to set foot on Texas soil? Well, truth told, nobody knows for sure. Apparently, though, the first English-speaker who left a record of his passage was a sailor named David Ingram, of the village of Barking in the county of Essex, east of 16th century London and today a suburb of the city.

We don't know much about David Ingram. We don't know who his parents were, where or when he was born or died, or where he is buried. We don't even know if his grave is marked—though it should be, and with a Texas historical marker. All we know for sure is that sometime around January of 1568 David Ingram and 113 other English sailors were set ashore about 30 miles north of Tampico, Mexico, and eleven months later David Ingram and two others showed up at Cape Breton, Newfoundland, on the Canadian mainland opposite the English colony of Nova Scotia or New Scotland, having walked more than 3000 miles.

In October of 1567 Sir John Hawkins, sea captain, set sail with six ships from the port of Plymouth, England to go to what later was known as Africa's "Slave Coast" to do some trading. Hawkins purchased six shiploads of slaves from the dominant tribes and sailed for South America.

Trade with Spanish America, particularly for the English, was strictly forbidden. The Spanish colonies, in fact, were forbidden by royal edict to trade with any country save Spain. All of which meant nothing at all to Hawkins, who knew very well that all he had to do was show up with merchandise the Spaniards wanted, grease a few palms, and sail home with a hold full of New World gold. One item the Spanish wanted a great deal was slaves.

Hawkins sold his shiploads of slaves for good Spanish-American gold, then set sail for home. Just as the ships were clearing the Caribbean they ran head-on into a real old-fashioned tropical storm. When the wind finally quit blowing, the six English ships were pretty badly damaged and only a few miles off the Mexican coast.

John Hawkins, like most 16th century English searovers, was—as far as the Spanish were concerned, at least—a pirate. Mexico was Spanish territory. England was, from time to time, at war with Spain—this voyage, in fact, was made just 21 years before the Spanish Armada sailed to invade England. Consequently, English ships and English sea captains weren't exactly welcome in the Caribbean Sea and Gulf of Mexico, which Spain considered a "Spanish lake."

Hawkins' ships were in serious need of repair and refitting, and the closest and best harbor was Vera Cruz. Thence Hawkins sailed, and his ships were refitted from Spanish stores. Somebody tipped off the government, and as the six English ships cleared the harbor, they were jumped by a squadron of Spanish men-of-war.

When the smoke cleared the English had won, if you want to call it that. They still had possession of Vera Cruz and the Spanish ships were gone, but four of Hawkins' ships were on the bottom and the harbor was full of Englishmen who were spitting salt water.

The two remaining ships were the *Judith* and the *Minion*. The *Judith*, commanded by a young man named Francis Drake—he'd make a real name for himself later—sailed for home and arrived without notable incident. The *Minion*, under Hawkins' personal command, picked up the survivors and then set out for England.

"With manie sorrowful heartes wee wandred in an unknowne Sea by ye space of fourteene dayes tyll hunger enforced us to seeke ye lande," Hawkins wrote. The *Minion* was badly overcrowded and underprovisioned. The sailors decided that "if they perished notte by drowning, yet hunger would inforce them to eatte one another." At their own request, 114 men were set ashore about 30 miles north of Tampico. They knew only that English possessions in the New World lay somewhere to the northeast.

In 1582 *Ye Relation* (story) *of David Ingram of Barking, in ye Countie of Essex, Sayler* (sailor)— Ingram by then being the last survivor—was published. It was a truly remarkable story—one of the greatest (and, today, the least known) adventure stories ever written.

Three sailors reached Canada. What became of the other 111 we don't know for sure. Some no doubt died of natural causes. Some were probably killed by Indians. Some may have gone native— many, many years later the first-generation offspring of brown-eyed Indian women and blue-eyed Americans sometimes had blue eyes, which is considered genetically impossible unless the women had blue-eyed ancestors and carried the recessive gene for blue eyes.

David Ingram's glowing description of the natural resources of what is now Texas has caused Dr. Thomas Cutrer, the historian of the English Texans, to call him "the first Texas braggart in the English tongue." According to Ingram, he saw "greate rockes of Chrystal, Rubies, being four inches long, and two inches broad." He also remarked on "a greate aboundance of Pearles" and "sundrie pieces of Golde some as bigge as a man's fist," and other mineral riches in profusion.

Ingram was a sailor. He wasn't a geologist or a jeweler. What might he have seen?

"Pearles" there were, and aplenty. The Texas coast produced pearls by the basketful, for the Karankawa Indians and later for the Spaniards, from native oyster beds that had been largely undisturbed almost since the beginning of time. The freshwater streams of Texas, in particular West Texas, abounded in fresh-water-pearl producing mussels. The Concho River near San Angelo was, until this century, famous for its fresh-water pearls. Ingram could very well have seen "an aboundance of Pearles."

How about those rubies? Well, it could depend on what you call "rubies." The "Black Prince Ruby," which is part of the British Crown Jewels, is actually a garnet, and—apart from its historical value, which makes it priceless—it's worth about

$500. You can find garnets—and sapphires as well, though not particularly large specimens of either, these days—in creeks in the granite hills not far west of Mason. As far as "Chrystal" goes, if you drive Texas 29 from Bartlett to Mason, as soon as you enter the granite hills between Barlett and Burnet you'll begin to see lots of "Chrystal"—veins of crystalline quartz from milky white to diamond clear, by the dozens—running through the rocks. And "Golde?" Remember, Ingram was a "sayler." Iron pyrite—"fool's gold"—in chunks "as bigge as a man's fist" isn't uncommon in the same area. Perhaps David Ingram wasn't "the first Texas braggart in the English tongue." Perhaps he was a simple sailor, reporting what he saw as he saw it.

"Greate rockes of chrystal . . . diamonds . . . ."
David Ingram

A vein of crystalline quartz, one of many in the granite hills, seams a granite outcropping on the north side of Texas 29, 5.5 miles west of the Texas 29/US 281 intersection in Burnet. Could this or a similar quartz vein be what an illiterate 16th century English "sayler" saw as "diamonds"?

Ingram also commented on "a greate plentie of Buffes (buffalo), Beares, Horses, Kine (cattle), Woolves, Foxes, Deare, Goates, Sheeps, Hares" (the jackrabbit is actually a hare, and Europeans have always made a distinction between hares and rabbits, though most Texas folks have always figured if a critter has long ears and jumps and it ain't a kangaroo, it's a rabbit and only a smart aleck would call it anything else), "and Conies" (rabbits). His *Relation* may be the earliest indication we have that there were wild horses and cattle in Texas, and would indicate that the Spaniards started losing horses and cattle much earlier than most historians think.

What the "sheeps" and "goates" may have been, if they were wild animals, is anybody's guess. While there were wild bighorn sheep in Texas until the late 19th century, they were much farther north than we have any reason to believe Ingram traveled. Oddly enough, though, the only wild animal akin to a goat in the Americas did live in Texas—but again far away from where Ingram appears to have wandered. It is kin to a goat—distantly—and closely kin to no other animal save itself on the face of the earth. Because it looked like and acted like what naturalists had identified as antelopes on other continents, we called it the "pronghorn antelope" in recognition that it alone, among antelopes, has a forked horn. When we later discovered that the "horn" is in fact an antler and is shed annually, the animal became even more confusing. Of course, when we finally met the only actual antelope native to the Americas it confused us even more—it looked, smelled, acted, and, when cooked, tasted like a goat, so we called it the Rocky Mountain Goat after the place we first found it.

Ingram mentioned seeing yet another animal, and that's caused a lot of folks to class him with Sir John Mandeville, Baron Munchausen, and Jim Bridger as a spinner of tall tales. David Ingram said he saw "olifants" in Texas. "Olifant," today, is spelled "elephant." David Ingram said he saw elephants in Texas.

Well, there were elephants—of a sort—in Texas. Once upon a time, anyway. That time, according to paleontologists, was no later than 10,000 years ago, not 400 years ago. Texas was home, once, to woolly mammoths and mastodons, and their skeletal remains are fairly common paleontological finds in the state. Most of us will recall that a huge deposit of mammoth and mastodon bones was found in downtown Austin while construction crews were excavating the foundations for a building on Congress Avenue.

David Ingram had been to Africa as a sailor. He probably knew an "olifant" when he saw an "olifant." What might he have seen in Texas that he would call an "olifant?"

The Osage Indians have tales of a mythical monster called "pasnuta." The Bidai, a Karankawan tribe that lived in Southeast Texas, had tales of a mythical monster they called "carancro." Both "pasnuta" and "carancro" were described, by old Indians who claimed to have seen the critters in person, as something very much like an elephant. Louis L'Amour, in his last western and final Sackett novel, *Jubal Sackett*, made use of the Osage "pasnuta" legend by having his hero meet and kill the last "pasnuta"—a woolly mammoth—in the Colorado/New Mexico/Arizona area.

Let's make something clear immediately— pasnuta and carancro have been called "mythical monsters" only because white men never saw them (or at least never saw them and lived to tell

about it). To the Indians neither pasnuta nor
carancro were mythical. They were big, nasty critters with bad habits, and—according to the
Indians—the last ones hadn't been dead all that
long when the first white men began showing up
in quantity about 1600. In addition, our unknown
explorers who left their record in the Sun-Hai
Ching also described a "monster" that could only
be some sort of elephant.

Did David Ingram, the first English-speaking
white man we know for sure walked in Texas,
actually see a living mammoth or mastodon—
perhaps even more than one—here in Texas in the
mid-1500s? We don't know and we'll probably
never know for sure, but old Davy seems to have
been a pretty accurate reporter of everything else
he saw.

THE FIRST TEXAS
REVOLUTION

At the beginning of the 19th century, Spain's overseas empire included not merely possessions in Africa and mainland Asia, but the Philippine Islands; all of South America except Brazil and three Alabama-sized chunks on the Caribbean coast that belonged to France, England, and The Netherlands; all of Central America except a Delaware-sized piece on the Honduran coast which belonged to England; all of Mexico; most of the islands of the Caribbean; and the present states of Texas, New Mexico, Arizona, Nevada, Colorado, California, and Utah, and parts of Oklahoma and Wyoming. Until Napoleon forced its cession to France in 1800, it had owned—for 37 years—the vast Louisiana Purchase territory which included at least Louisiana, Arkansas, Missouri, Iowa, Kansas, Nebraska, Minnesota, and the Dakotas and could have been considered to include the rest of Wyoming, Montana, Idaho, Oregon, and part of Washington as well.

That was as of January 1, 1801. When the 20th century actually dawned—on January 1, 1901—Spain had lost all its New World empire and the Philippines as well. It had, primarily, the United

States to blame. By revolting against colonial rule from England, the new nation of the United States lit a flame that still burns brightly, and it has lighted not merely revolts against colonial rulers the world over, but revolts against oppressive home regimes as well.

Most of these revolts were true revolutions, or at least started that way. A good many of them, however, got sidetracked. The French Revolution, which was intended to produce a new European "America," degenerated into a terrorist state that eventually fell to an internal tyrant named Napoleon Bonaparte. The Russian Revolution was seized by a cadre of highly trained and close-knit totalitarians which produced, instead of freedom, a regime far more oppressive than the one that preceded it.

The revolution which began in Mexico on La Noche del Grito—which was, by the way, the night of September 15, not "la noche de diez y seis"—was an exception. It was by no means a "revolt of the people." It was, instead, essentially a squabble between two groups of aristocrats to decide which one would get to be big pig at the trough in stealing anything worth stealing.

English and French settlement in the New World was handled on what were basically libertarian principles. Colonists went in pretty much on their own, and where they went, what they did, where they claimed and built, and who handled local government was decided locally. In the old frontier expression, they "hoed their own corn."

Spanish colonies were settled more on the lines of a feudal society. Everything, in essence, was directed from Spain. Officials sent from Spain ruled every moment of daily life, whether it was connected with the church or the civil government. Spain, either directly or through appointees, ruled everything from who could take off into the wilderness to hunt for gold or souls to where a town could be built, the plan the town had to take, how many people could live in it, and what its governmental form would be. Every detail had to be cleared, ultimately, with the king, and this meant wading through layer after layer of bureaucrats, from the local alcalde all the way to the throne room.

It could take as much as two years for a request to get all the way to the king and back, and even the most urgent necessities—like building a military outpost to get warning of Indian raids— had to go through the whole process. Nobody dared do anything on his own, because if he did and the request to do it came back disapproved— no matter how necessary it had been to do it —everybody involved was liable to prosecution. This could amount to a fine, confiscation of property, imprisonment, or even execution—or any combination of the above or all of them.

With all these levels of bureaucracy to wade through, there was—as you might well imagine— an almost unlimited opportunity for graft. At every level of government, from the local alcalde to the throne room itself, la mordita—the little bite, the Spanish slang term for bribery—was a way of life. Nothing moved, nothing was acted on, nothing was forwarded, nothing got done unless it was "greased through the machinery" with money. Obviously, the higher up in the bureaucracy an official was, the more "little bites" he got to take, and the fatter his wallet got.

A bureaucrat stood to make lots of money this way. His salary, in fact, was minimal—the Spanish term for "salary" was "hardship," and it was well applied—and nobody could live on such a salary. It was expected that a bureaucrat would live on bribes. That way he didn't take much directly out of the royal pocketbook. A low-level bureaucrat got the mordita only out of the pockets of the locals. An upper-level bureaucrat—say, on a provincial level—got mordita from all the towns in his province. The higher up the bureaucratic ladder, the more mordita added up. That fact, in essence, led directly to the 1810 revolution.

Only aristocrats got to serve in the bureaucracy, at least in those places where it was possible to acquire the proceeds of mordita, and in New Spain there were two types of aristocrats—españoles and criollos. An español was a person of "pure Spanish blood"—that might well be a mixture of native Iberian, Roman, Greek, Carthaginian, Levantine, Goth, Gaul, Visigoth, Teuton, Celt, Vandal, Hun, and several dozen varieties of North African Arab including Berber, Taureg, and Moor—who happened to have been born in Spain. A criollo was a person of "pure Spanish blood" who happened to have been born in the New World. In the way the government of New Spain was set up, criollos—no matter how ancient and exalted their Spanish lineage might be—got only the lowest-level (and therefore lowest-paying) bureaucratic appointments, regardless of how talented they might be. The big money always went to españoles.

This, as you might expect, got under the criollos' skin in a big way. They wanted a bigger slice of the pie and if they could get it, they wanted the whole pie to themselves. The españoles weren't about to give it to them.

Had this condition not existed, Padre Hidalgo would be a tiny footnote in the history of Spanish America instead of a national hero of Mexico. Hidalgo's revolt was initially aimed at the bureaucracy—all of it, españoles and criollos alike—and in the famous grito (yell) he included the words "viva el Rey Fernando"—"Long live King Ferdinand."

The Spanish-Mexican peasantry, most of them mestizos—"mixed bloods" who were part Spanish and part Indian—who first rallied to Hidalgo, were virtually unarmed. Unlike English and French settlers, Spanish settlers—unless they were part of the "aristocracy"—were not permitted to own and keep firearms, not even for their own defense. All defense—against Indians, criminals, and outside invaders—was the province of the army, and in most cases the army was so inefficient, poorly armed, poorly mounted, and corrupt that it was hard put to defend itself, let alone those it had the responsibility of defending. Hidalgo's mestizo followers simply didn't have the wherewithal to make a revolution—but the criollos did.

What began as a revolt against corruption, then, degenerated into a fight between two extremely corrupt factions over the right to steal. The situation was ripe for a true revolutionary idealist with an armed backing—or an imposter posing as a true idealist—to move in. This led to what is called, in Texas history, the Gutiérrez-Magee Filibuster, the Gutiérrez-Magee Expedition, the Green Flag Revolt, or the First Texas Revolution.

In 1763, following the Seven Years' War, France ceded the Louisiana Territory to Spain. Spain ruled the settled parts of it for 37 years, and in New Orleans you will find a Spanish-built building called "The Cabildo," in which the Spanish town council or cabildo met. If you read very closely into New Orleans and Louisiana history, you will find that a much-beloved Spanish priest, who remained after Louisiana returned to French rule and stayed on under American rule, was found, after his death, to have come to establish in New Orleans the dreaded Spanish Inquisition, with all the horrors associated with it. In Missouri you will find a town called New Madrid (they pronounce it MAD-rid) which was established as Nueva Madrid.

In 1800 Napoleon Bonaparte forced Spain to return the Louisiana territory to France, and in 1803 he sold it, lock, stock, and barrel, to Thomas Jefferson's United States. That put the upstart country that had started all this revolutionary trouble right at New Spain's back door.

The exact boundary between Louisiana and New Spain had never been settled. As far back as the very early 1700s, Los Adaes, which is only six miles from present-day Robeline, Louisiana, was the official Spanish capital of what would later become Texas; and Natchitoches, on the Red River, was a Spanish town originally. (Natchitoches and Nacogdoches, by the way, are the same Indian word—spelled by a Frenchman and by a Spaniard. For that matter Ouachita, Wichita, and Washita are the same Indian word—spelled by Frenchmen and two Americans who heard the word differently. Oueco, Hueco, Huaco, and Waco follow the same pattern.) The Spanish claimed the line of the Red and Calcasieu rivers as the boundary, while the Americans claimed the Sabine. An agreement was reached by which the Spaniards, while claiming the Red/Calcasieu river line, would pull back west of the Sabine, while the Americans, still claiming the Sabine, would go no farther west than the Red/Calcasieu line. The area between was called the Neutral Strip, and neither country was supposed to send armed forces into it. As you might expect, the Neutral Strip became a haven for outlaws and a staging area for criminals of every description.

There is not enough difference between José Bernardo Macimiliano Gutiérrez de Lara and Antonio López de Santa Anna y Pérez de LeBron to shake a stick at. Both were treacherous, vicious, murderous dictators. Gutiérrez de Lara was no revolutionary idealist who wanted the blessings of liberty for his countrymen and their children, he was a would-be dictator who wanted to carve a personal empire for himself and his pals out of the ruins of Spanish power in North America. He was also an excellent actor and a fantastically convincing liar. That is part and parcel of the saga of the Green Flag.

Bernardo Gutiérriez de Lara started out as a blacksmith and tradesman in the town Revilla, along the Rio Grande, and he seems to have been one of the driving forces behind the revolution there. In 1811 he was chased out of Revilla by the advance of the Spanish army, and he began to flee eastward. Early on the morning of September 17, 1811, he entered the Neutral Strip—with Spanish troops and agents hot on his heels.

Gutiérrez de Lara escaped the Spanish agents and entered official United States Territory the following day. From then until August of 1812 he busied himself gathering support and money to "bring freedom to the people of Texas"—a cause which the United States largely supported, in part, at least, because La Salle's claiming of Texas had made the land at least nominally part of Louisiana. When the United States purchased the Louisiana Territory from the French, the French claimed the purchase included Texas. The United States knew better; Texas was and had always been Spanish territory, but France did have a slim and doubtful—but quasilegal—claim to the territory that the United States might some day find it convenient to assert.

Gutiérrez de Lara was by no means alone in the States. At the same time, though not necessarily acting in concert with him, was a Spanish officer who supported the revolution, José Álvarez de Toledo. As you might expect, Gutiérrez de Lara's call for help also attracted some Americans, one of whom was 2nd Lieutenant Augustus William Magee, U. S. Army, a West Point graduate of considerable ability and of Irish ancestry. Another was Samuel Kemper, another Irish-American, who had already fought against Spain in Florida. The man designated "quartermaster-general" of Gutiérrez de Lara's army was yet a third Irishman, Samuel Davenport, who had held Spanish citizen-ship since 1794 and had done very well for himself with a Spanish-granted Indian-trader's license at Natchitoches.

The flag chosen for the First Republic of Texas was solid green. Why green? It had no particular significance to Mexican Texas—but a green flag had a lot of significance to Irishmen. Ireland, a Catholic country under Protestant English rule since the days of Queen Elizabeth I, was a living hell for its own people. Could the Irish among Gutiérrez de Lara's army have been intending to establish a new Ireland in already-Catholic Mexico—a refuge for the Irish, persecuted and dying in their homeland—far across the sea and out of reach of England? This has never been proved, but the presence of a large number of Irish-Americans in Gutiérrez de Lara's army and the selection of a flag that was Ireland's national color might tend to indicate something of the sort.

The United States did not actively support Gutiérrez de Lara, but it also didn't actively discourage his recruiting efforts. If anything his recruiting of an army, the training of it by Magee, and the purchase of arms, ammunition, and supplies for it were made a lot easier than they might have been by various governmental officials who were personally sympathetic to the cause of Mexican independence—and just possibly the adding of Texas to the United States.

Southerners in particular were anxious to add Texas—being south of Mason and Dixon's line, it would be a slave state, therefore aiding the South. With a large and prosperous agricultural economy largely dependent upon slave labor but with much smaller overall population than the North, the South was hopelessly outnumbered in the U.S. House of Representatives. In the Senate, where each state regardless of size or population was equally represented, there was a precarious balance between the small but numerous Northern states and the much larger, less numerous Southern ones. The addition of the vast expanse of Texas as a territory, which could then be divided into six or seven new slave states, was very attractive to the South.

Gutiérrez de Lara's machinations had not gone unnoticed west of the Sabine. He had, in fact, been propagandizing most of Texas with a pamphlet called "The Friend of Men," written by José Álvarez de Toledo. In it, the writer called on "the sons of Montezuma" to "shake off the barbarous and ignominious yoke" of Spanish domination and choose for themselves the type of government they wanted—which, as it turned out, was just about the exact opposite of what José Bernardo Macimiliano Gutiérrez de Lara had in mind. The rumor spread among the revolutionists along the border that Gutiérrez de Lara and Toledo were poised in Louisiana with an army of fifteen thousand Americans and Mexicans and eight thousand Indians, prepared to strike into Texas when the time was ripe.

It was not until August 7, 1812, that the Green Flag finally entered Texas. The advance guard of what was called The Republican Army of the North—which totaled more like 500 than 23,000 men, about 95 percent of them Americans, with practically no Indians at all, at least not at first—under Sam Kemper's command crossed the Sabine headed for Spanish Texas' main outpost east of the Colorado, Nacogdoches. It met, almost immediately, a mule train loaded with wool and silver, commanded by a Spanish army colonel named Zambrano. Zambrano had about 300 mules and 100 "armed" muleskinners, but to the Spanish way of thinking "armed" might mean "he's got a machete someplace if he can find it." The result was predictable—the poorly armed muleskinners came nose to nose with Kentucky, Tennessee, Arkansas, and Mississippi backwoodsmen armed with long rifles, and those who lived through it headed for the tall timber. They did, though, manage to take their mules with them, so Kemper didn't get the shipment of coined silver they carried.

The next morning the rest of the army, under Magee, crossed the Sabine and took up the chase. On August 10 Gutiérrez de Lara, who was waiting at Natchitoches, got word that his army was in Texas and left to join it. William Shaler, who was Gutiérrez de Lara's host—and the president's watchdog—reported in a letter that when he left Natchitoches, Gutiérrez de Lara seemed to be greatly afraid that his enterprise would fail. If he was, he was about the only person involved with it who was worried.

Zambrano and his party hightailed it for Nacogdoches, and about 25 miles to the east he left a rear guard of twenty men. At dawn on August 11 Kemper and the Republican advance guard surprised and captured them all and either deliberately released or "allowed to escape" one of their number. He reached Nacogdoches that night with word that Gutiérrez de Lara was coming with 700 Americans—which was an exaggeration—but had no intention of bothering any ordinary citizen, harming any property, or interfering with anyone's religion. Later that evening a second fugitive/messenger turned up with word that another thousand Americans would shortly land at Matagorda Bay.

The Spanish commandant at Nacogdoches, Montero, sounded the alarm—and nothing happened. Nacogdoches folks didn't really love the Spanish anyway, having been ordered several times to abandon their town and possessions by royal decree. Nobody—neither the citizens nor the local militia—turned out.

Montero paraded the local regular garrison and ordered the militia out, then set out—not for the approaching enemy, but for San Antonio de Bejar. A militia captain immediately called a halt, and all of the militia and all but ten of the regular soldiers deserted and went back to their homes and families in Nacogdoches. Zambrano and Montero, together with a few of Zambrano's muleskinners and the ten remaining soldiers, set out for San Antonio. Zambrano left his cargo—including the minted silver—behind.

Nacogdoches got a welcoming committee together and received the Republican Army of the North with open arms. The town turned over its archives and public property, including all the guns and powder the army left behind, lots of food, a quantity of spears and lances, and 600 horses and mules. In addition, the newcomers got everything on Zambrano's mule train—80,000 pounds of fine wool and the entire load of silver coin. The total take was estimated at $60,000—in a day when bullion gold sold for $10 per troy ounce.

At this point Gutiérrez de Lara and the Republican Army of the North owned all of Texas east of the La Bahía/Bejar line. There was nothing to oppose them, and the only important Spanish town in that part of Texas had not just surrendered, it had pretty well signed up for the fight on the Green Flag side.

Manuel de Salcedo, the Spanish governor in San Antonio, yelled for some help from the other side of the Rio Grande. Specifically, he asked the viceroy in Mexico City for one thousand soldiers. "If this is not done," he wrote to the viceroy, "Texas faces a more formidable insurrection than that of 1811, since the people easily embrace sedition, believing the Americans, who claim they come not to injure the inhabitants but to aid them in winning independence. They do not realize, as I, that the Americans, under the pretext of liberty, are working to take possession of Texas." He also sent appeals to governors and military commanders in Camargo, Monterrey, Coahuila, and San Luis Potosi.

Governor Cordero, in Coahuila, sent one company of troops. The other governors and military commanders sent excuses. The viceroy didn't even bother to reply for nearly seven months, and then he said "no troops."

At first, the Republican Army consolidated itself in Nacogdoches and opened a thriving trade with Natchitoches, on the east edge of the Neutral Strip. Davenport, who didn't lose any money in the process, supplied the troops with food, saddles, more and better powder—Spanish powder was generally of pretty poor quality—gunflints, lead, and uniforms, including a gaudy, embroidered one for Gutiérrez de Lara. Governor

Claiborne of Louisiana proclaimed the Neutrality Law, which—at least it was supposed to—prohibited Louisiana from being a staging area for the invasion of Spanish territory. It was ignored.

Newspapers in Tennessee, Kentucky, Louisiana, Mississippi—even as far away as Georgia and Ohio—issued calls for volunteers to "fight for liberty for Texas." By harvest time Mississippi and Louisiana had been so thoroughly drained of excess manpower that farmers who didn't own slaves couldn't find anyone to hire to get the crops in—they'd all gone to Texas.

Augustus Magee seems to have been a superb soldier—not just a fighting soldier, but an organizing one as well. He organized his 450 or so Americans into five companies and made a mounted company of the Spanish regulars who'd deserted to the Republican side. He also stationed "welcoming committees" just on the west side of the Sabine. Instead of letting groups of incomers plunder their way across to Nacogdoches, they were signed up, organized into companies, and marched into town in a soldierly fashion. This was a major surprise to the Spanish inhabitants, who'd been used to their own soldiers looting them anytime they felt like it, and who'd been told that the Americans were coming to rape, loot, burn, murder, and destroy.

Magee's discipline of his little army made a very favorable impression on the locals wherever it went—and Gutiérrez de Lara either kept silent or mouthed the platitudes of liberty at every opportunity. Magee, though the actual commander of troops, styled himself only colonel. Kemper was named major, and four Americans—Perry, Ross, Lockett, and Hall—became the captains. Gutiérrez de Lara was styled commander in chief and had a fancy embroidered suit to prove it, but he had little to do with the actual running of the army.

Magee sent scouts on ahead to the village of Trinidad, on the Trinity River, and found that Montero and Zambrano were there—and that the local garrison consisted of a Regular Spanish Army captain and 37 soldiers, most of whom were effectively unarmed. Montero and Zambrano saw the Americans enter the town to a welcome and realized that the soldiers in Trinidad, most of whom were in rags, poorly fed, and hadn't been paid in a long time, weren't in any mood to support the king. They moved about 50 miles to the west—minus five more soldiers, who deserted to the Republicans—and sent word to Salcedo about what was happening. He said "come on," so they—and their tiny remaining group—went on to Bejar.

The most effective weapon in a revolutionist's arsenal is not a gun, but a printing press. Gutiérrez de Lara knew it, got one, and knew very well how to use it.

So far the Green Flag revolt had been bloodless—only a few shots had been fired. Gutiérrez de Lara wanted to keep it that way as long as possible. From Nacogdoches he began to bombard La Bahía and Bejar—the only two remaining towns of any size in Texas—with bombastic proclamations from "General Headquarters, Nacogdoches, September 1, 1812, in the Second Year of Our Independence" and signed by "José Bernardo Macimiliano Gutiérrez de Lara, Colonel in the Armies of the Republic of Mexico, Deputy for that Republic in the United States of America, and Commander-in-chief of the Army of the North."

According to Gutiérrez de Lara the Americans came not as looters, ravishers of womanhood, and thieves of land as the Spanish government painted them, but as idealistic revolutionaries whose only

thought was to enable their brethren west of the
Sabine to enjoy the same blessings of liberty they
themselves had won at great cost. He didn't, however, bother to mention how much land and what
riches he'd promised the Americans they could
have if they came. The promises totalled $400 in
cash—a lot of money with gold at $10 per ounce—
and a league of land (about 4400 acres) for each
volunteer. Gutiérrez de Lara, typically, didn't say
where he was going to get the money and the land.

One of the proclamations was addressed to "Officers, Soldiers, and Inhabitants of San Antonio de
Bejar." It exhorted them to rise up against the yoke
of Spanish oppression and join with the army of
Americans, descendants of those who had won
America's independence from British rule, who
were marching to secure for the people of Texas
the same rights they had won for their own people
from the British. Others, addressed to "Beloved,
Honorable Compatriots who reside in the
Province of Texas," described Gutiérrez de Lara's
efforts on their behalf in the United States—and
spared no self-praise whatever—and to the people
of Mexico proper, telling them that the Army of
the North came not to rob, but to join with them
in securing economic and political liberty.

He also issued a proclamation filled with praise
to the American volunteers in Nacogdoches,
which assured them that in giving Mexico an independent government they would also assure
themselves possession of the lands they had been
promised, the rights to work and profit from any
gold or silver mines they might discover, and the
right to capture and sell any wild horses or mules
they might find. In addition, it said that once the
expenses of the expedition itself had been paid,
the confiscated property of the Royalists would be
divided among them and they would also get

money from the treasury of the government to be
established. These things he didn't bother to include in the proclamations to his countrymen, but
he covered all the bases.

Most of these proclamations were sent by
courier from Nacogdoches to La Bahía and Bejar.
At least three of the couriers were captured, and
two of them were executed in the plaza militario
in Bejar, but that was about all the success the
Royalists could claim. Proclamations got through,
people read them, and revolt simmered. Manuel
de Salcedo got no help from across the river. On
September 13 the Army of the North—only 600
strong but well-equipped, well-armed, and expert-
ly trained by Augustus Magee—left Nacogdoches
for Trinidad. At the same time Salcedo, hearing of
it, pulled in his outposts to Bejar and prepared to
make a stand. By October 12 Magee had an
advance guard twelve miles west of the Trinity,
and the invasion of Texas by the Green Flag had
begun in earnest. Gutiérrez issued yet another
proclamation, declaring Texas an independent
republic from the Sabine to the Trinity.

Meanwhile James Monroe, president of the
United States, was playing both ends against the
middle. While Shaler, in Natchitoches, was to be
the president's liason with Gutiérrez and Magee,
he sent Dr. John Hamilton Robinson to Bejar to
assure Salcedo that the United States had no
territorial designs on Texas and was not aiding the
revolutionists. This, of course, was a bald-faced
lie—the United States was openly aiding the
revolutionists in getting arms and supplies and
turning a blind eye to the steady stream of reinforcements that was crossing the Neutral Strip in
direct violation of both U.S. and Spanish law and
any number of treaties. Monroe, too, was covering
all bases—he intended to maintain good relations

with both sides until somebody won, at which point the United States would have a solid foothold in the memories of whoever ruled Texas.

Salcedo had, indeed, pulled in his outposts. There was only a small garrison at La Bahía, and when the Green Flag army marched into the town on November 7, 1812, the garrison fled while the inhabitants welcomed the Republican army with food and flowers. The catch was, Salcedo wasn't waiting at Bejar. He'd advanced to the Guadalupe, where he intended to fight a pitched battle. Without realizing he was there, the Republicans flanked him and took the second strongest fortification in Texas without a fight.

Salcedo and Simón de Herrera, his military commander, then decided to attack the La Bahía presidio. On November 10 they did—with no success at all. The Republicans had food, water, powder, lead—and the sympathies if not the active support of the local people. The Royalists laid seige to the fort.

The Republicans had the fort. The Royalists shortly had the town. The Americans had been promised that the citizens of Texas would rise up and welcome them with open arms. Here they were, instead, with muskets at the ready, beseiging the would-be liberators. Magee, Kemper, and the Americans called a council of war. Gutiérrez was not included.

On November 23 the Americans met with Salcedo and Herrera. They represented that they had been deceived by Gutiérrez de Lara. They offered to return to the United States and in no way further molest Spanish Texas—if the Spaniards would agree to give a full pardon to and arrange protection for the Mexican Republicans who would have to stay behind. This guarantee Salcedo could not give, and no agreement was reached. That afternoon the Royalists once more assaulted the walls and were driven back with considerable losses and no success whatever. Once again the two forces settled into a state of seige.

The seige of the presidio at La Bahía is the longest known seige in Texas history—while the seige at the Alamo lasted only 13 days, the La Bahía seige of 1812-1813 lasted four months. It was also one of the most peculiar seiges in the history of warfare.

The object of the game, in seige warfare, is to surround your enemy's fortification, cut it off from all support and resupply, and then wait until starvation and disease force it to surrender or you can get somebody inside—through treachery or whatever—to open the gates so you can take it by storm. In order to do that, you need to outnumber the people you beseige, cut off their supplies while maintaining your own, and cut them off from all hope. About all the Spanish ever managed to do was to outnumber the besieged forces, and not by all that much.

From time to time the Royalists would attempt to attack, and the Republicans would whip the attackers soundly. Royalist troops deserted almost daily, and a good many of them joined the beseiged Republicans. Scouting parties from the Republicans ranged as far as the Nueces River. When they returned they brought cattle and game meat, and the Royalists were unable to stop them. Recruits from the States penetrated Royalist lines and joined the Republicans inside the fort. The Royalists, in the meantime, weren't getting resupplied, and were losing men by the day.

Augustus Magee, who was the only really competent military commander the Republicans had at La Bahía, had been sick since the troops left Trinidad. On February 6, 1813, he died at La Bahía and was buried with military honors inside the fort's walls. Though the exact location of his grave is not known, a U.S. military tombstone has been erected just outside the present administration building of the presidio-museum. It is inscribed with his name and dates. The death of Magee almost ended the Republican resistance—but not quite.

Samuel Kemper was appointed to replace Magee. While Sam was a fighting man, he was by no means the efficient, organized soldier Magee was, and the little army was to miss Magee sorely.

About the time Magee died, the Royalists made one final effort to take the fort by storm. In an all-day fight that left the ground around the walls littered with Royalist corpses, it failed. Salcedo and Herrera were without powder, their men were virtually in rags, desertion—largely to the Republicans, who were eating well—was rampant, and the Royalists were almost without food. On February 19, 1813, the Royalists lifted the seige and started the long march back to San Antonio, carrying their wounded and losing men right and left to desertion. In addition, the news that the Republicans had withstood the seige spread, and not only did Bahía welcome them with open arms, the people of Bejar prepared to welcome them as liberators.

The Royalists got nothing but bad news. Cordero sent word he was sending forty men, ten boxes of powder, and a box of lead. Bustamante told the viceroy that he had few troops and fewer supplies, but that he might be able to make a show of force at the Rio Grande, or he might be able to join Salcedo in prolonging the seige at Bahía. The captain at Camargo reported that all over his area the people were in revolt, that revolutionists were raiding ranchos of Royalists and taking cattle and hostages. Mier, Refugio, Reynosa, and Laredo, he reported, openly favored the revolution, and in Reynosa people were openly talking of revolt. If the Republicans advanced toward Camargo, he felt his best course was to retreat into the interior to prevent any deserters from his own ranks from swelling the Republican army.

Rumors in Mexico and Bejar had it that the Republicans had 14,000 men, including several thousand Indians, and were actually marching on Bejar. The total strength of the Republican army in Texas at the time was about 550 men, with no Indians at all. Indians were raiding around Bejar, however, and by reports had murdered 55 people and stolen 5,000 sheep and 10,000 horses and mules while the seige at Bahía was on.

In the midst of all this, Gutiérrez de Lara sent a messenger all the way back to Natchitoches. The purpose was to tell the Republicans' supporters that the road to Bahía was open, that Texas—except for Bejar, upon which the Republicans intended to move shortly—was in Republican hands, that any materials for the army that came in would be admitted duty-free, and that a port would shortly be opened at Matagorda Bay. On March 12 the messenger returned to Bahía with about forty or fifty more Americans and somewhere around 100 Indians who'd decided to join the fight. On the 19th, the Republican army set out to take Bejar.

Along Salado Creek, five leagues—about 13 miles—from the heart of San Antonio, Salcedo and Herrera planned a surprise. They were entrenched on high ground along the creek with somewhere around 1200 soldiers and six cannon. The ambush, though, was spotted, and in what is known today as "The Battle of the Salado" (or the Battle of Rosalis) the Royalists were routed, leaving over

100 men dead on the field and abandoning all their baggage and their artillery.

The Republicans advanced to within one league (2.5 miles) of San Antonio at the Concepcion mission, where they went to camp and prepared to storm the city. Sam Kemper, now colonel in actual command of the army, raided the town corral, capturing all the guards and taking about 3,000 horses—which effectively set the entire Royalist presence in Texas afoot. These successes encouraged the people of Bejar, and day by day the Republican ranks swelled as citizens, deserting militia, and deserting soldiers from Salcedo's small force joined the revolutionists.

On the morning of April 1 Sam Kemper led his little army to the very gates of the city. Salcedo sent a flag of truce and a list of conditions under which he would surrender. Three of them were human-itarian conditions—he requested that the city not be looted, that the people not be required to give up their arms, religion, property, or privileges and that no taxes be imposed, and that the sick and wounded be cared for. The other nine conditions were pretty sassy for a feller who'd gotten whip-ped every time he met the Republican army and had just gotten through getting his behind kicked every step of the way from Goliad to San Antone. Among other demands, he wanted his soldiers, together with all their weapons—including artil-lery—baggage, ammunition, and provisions to be allowed to leave Texas unmolested, along with any inhabitants who wanted to do so—they were sup-posed to be able to take all their personal belongings, livestock, and treasure with them— and the Spanish officials in Texas were not to be mistreated. While Kemper and Gutiérrez de Lara agreed to the humanitarian demands, they refused the rest. After a day of blustering and threats on both sides, Salcedo and Herrera agreed to an unconditional surrender, with the understanding that the humanitarian aspect of Salcedo's demands would be respected.

The surrender itself was a drama. Salcedo offered his sword to Kemper and the Americans, but they refused it—the nominal commander in chief was Gutiérrez de Lara. Salcedo refused to hand his sword to the man he considered an upstart and a criminal. Instead he rammed the point in the ground and stepped back. Gutiérrez de Lara took up the sword, but the insult was a mortal one.

On April 1, 1813, Texas became a republic in fact. There were no Spanish troops under arms anywhere north of the Rio Grande. The Green Flag went up over the Governor's Palace in San Antonio, the officers of the Spanish army were made prisoners, any Spanish soldier who refused to join the Republicans was disarmed, and the jails were opened to free political prisoners—and, as usually happens in such cases, not a few common criminals masquerading as political prisoners. Then José Bernardo Macimiliano Gutiérrez de Lara began to show his true colors.

On the evening of April 3 Antonio Delgado, commanding 100 local militiamen, rode out of San Antonio, ostensibly to escort Manuel de Salcedo and thirteen other Spanish officers to the coast, where they were expected to take ship for Mexico. Salcedo, who was a true gentleman of the old school, had endeared himself to the Americans through his concern for the welfare of his people in San Antonio. Herrera, who had fought his battles hard but in a chivalrous manner, was equally well-liked by the Americans.

What Delgado—with the full knowledge and connivance of Gutiérrez de Lara—intended was nothing less than cold-blooded murder. Six miles south of San Antonio the fourteen Spaniards were thrown off their horses and stripped naked, their throats were cut, and their bodies were mutilated. The bodies were left unburied on the ground. The next morning the detachment rode back into Bejar and began to brag about the killings.

The Americans were horrified and angered. Though Delgado insisted that he was justified—so he said, his brother and father had been executed by Salcedo for the crimes of possessing revolutionist literature and expressing revolutionary sentiments—the Americans had caught the first glimpse of what "freedom" really meant in Gutiérrez de Lara's terms, and it disgusted them. A party of Americans went to find the bodies and buried them properly. Immediately afterwards, a number of Americans simply quit and went home, refusing to support the sort of government that murdered chivalrous enemies.

The "constitution" which Gutiérrez de Lara proclaimed was far from what he'd talked about in the United States. If anything, the government he established in Texas was more repressive than the Spanish regime. The "President-Protector"— Gutiérrez de Lara, of course—was an effectual dictator and retained the power to appoint and fire any and all legislators. When the Americans objected that this wasn't what they meant when they said "freedom," Gutiérrez de Lara smiled and replied that his people "weren't ready for American-style freedom yet." A good many more Americans, disgusted to find that instead of freeing Mexico from a tyrant, they had simply aided in a transfer of power from one tyrant to another, quit and went home.

Gutiérrez de Lara's form of government increasingly angered the Americans, who—in ones and twos—began to drift away, particularly since the promised money and land grants hadn't materialized. Sam Kemper, the only American leader most of the Americans trusted, asked for—and was given—furlough and went to Louisiana, never to return. Spanish leaders emerged—one was José Álvarez de Toledo, who was a Spanish officer well-trained in the arts of war. Another, Miguel Menchaca, a tall, handsome, blue-eyed, blondhaired man who looked like a leader was supposed to look, acquitted himself well in a skirmish with a Royalist probe at Alazan and became the local hero.

Gutiérrez de Lara, meanwhile, was losing ground. Though he was something of a local hero, his governmental policies and his vacillating over the distribution of the promised money and land to the Americans were losing the army its fighting men. While Gutiérrez and his long-time revolutionary credentials were extremely popular in Bexar, his acts were costing his government the thing it needed most to keep the revolution going—fighting men who knew what they were doing. On August 6 Gutiérrez was deposed and Toledo placed in charge of the government as well as the army.

While Gutiérrez was personally popular, Toledo—for all his competence—was not. Menchaca disliked Toledo both because Menchaca was a Gutiérrez partisan and because Menchaca—who had natural leadership ability but no experience in warfare whatever—wanted to command the army. The locals disliked Toledo because he was a gachupin—an aristocrat they viewed as a man who'd turned his coat against the king and might turn it against them.

Far to the south of the Rio Grande the Spanish Royalist government finally awakened to the fact that something very disturbing was happening in the far-away province of Texas and determined to do something about it. Jose Joaquín Arredondo, an extremely competent soldier—and a man with an almost unbelieveable capacity for cruelty—was appointed to retake Texas for the Crown. In early August, after an abortive probe that ended in a Republican victory at Alazan, Arredondo came north in force. His advance was spotted, and on August 19, Toledo, with about 1400 men—local militia, former Spanish Royalist soldiers, Americans, and Indians—set out to meet him.

The Green Flag Republic lasted four months and eighteen days, then died in the bloodiest single day of battle ever fought on Texas soil: the Battle of El Encinal de Medina, usually—and incorrectly—called The Battle of the Medina. The battle took place in a sandy post-oak thicket (an encinal) in the northeast corner of present Atascosa County, over twenty miles from the Medina River (and from the Texas historical marker that commemorates it).

There are about as many tales of how the battle was lost as there are people to tell them, but for years Arredondo has been given credit for much more tactical expertise than he really had, and Toledo has been condemned for falling into a well-set trap that "he should have seen coming." According to standard historical sources, Arredondo sent out an advance guard, which Toledo attacked and chased. The advance guard was bait for a classic killing-ground ambush, and when the Republican army chased the bait between the two wings of Arredondo's force, the slaughter began.

Based on more recent research, that isn't what happened. It was a blazing hot August day and both sides were exhausted from the heat. The

Republicans encountered an advance guard, beat it handily, and went looking for water, which was rumored to be available in El Encinal de Medina. Breathing the sulfur-laden smoke of black powder brings on a powerful thirst—as any reenactor can tell you these days.

At about the time the Republicans entered the encinal—a post-oak thicket on sandy ground—from the north, the Royalists entered from the south, and the two armies met in the extremely close and confusing terrain. What has been called a "battle" was in fact a series of small, vicious hand-to-hand fights in the timber, with—considering the close terrain and the fog of powdersmoke that hung over any 19th century battlefield—no small group being able to be sure what any other small group was doing.

In the midst of the fighting, Menchaca, who was the only leader the locals would follow, was hit in the neck with what was described as "a cannonball." (Those who recall the discovery of what may have been Menchaca's grave, on Blue Wing Road in Bexar County, may also recall that the skeleton had a 1 ½" ball buried in its neck vertebrae.) With the fall of their leader, the locals began to retreat in confusion, leaving the Americans and Indians to face the Spanish alone.

The Indians promptly disappeared—pitched battles were definitely not their preferred style of fighting—and the Americans, badly outnumbered, found themselves alone on the battlefield. The American resistance broke and the men scattered. Nearly 1,400 casualties—American, local, Indian, and Spanish—were counted on the battlefield by Arredondo's staff.

José Joaquín Arredondo was no Salcedo. He showed no mercy. Any wounded rebels found on the field were bayoneted or sabered to death on the spot, their bodies stripped and dismembered, and body parts hung from trees all the way back to San Antonio.

The locals were the first to reach San Antonio, and—like fugitives everywhere—spread panic when they arrived. Within a few hours nearly 300 San Antonians—the most vocal and outspoken Republicans who could hope for no mercy whatever—were fleeing east with what they could carry.

Arredondo entered Bejar on August 19, and between then and September 3 he executed by firing squad or beheading—and without trial—at least 327 people. In every case confession and last rites were denied to the condemned. Instead they were dismembered and hung from trees and buildings around San Antonio. He also arrested the wives, widows, and physically mature daughters of every rebel he could identify. They were confined to a local prison called La Quinta, which he set up. During the day they were forced to grind corn and make tortillas for his army, and during the night they were parceled out as concubines to the Royalist soldiers. The officer in charge of the prison detail—who went about his chores with great delight—was a young lieutenant named Antonio López de Santa Anna y Pérez de LeBrón. The younger children of the families were turned out onto the streets, their homes taken as quarters by the army. They were forbidden to beg, and anyone caught giving them food or money was publicly whipped. Survivors lived by picking through garbage heaps and eating what they could find.

Arredondo didn't forget the ones who fled, either. He sent his cavalry commander, Colonel Ignacio Elizondo, in pursuit of them. Elizondo swept East Texas with a fury, capturing and shooting over 100 men, and making prisoners of nearly

100 men, women, and children. He finally stopped
at Trinidad, having been informed by a messenger
that all the people of Nacogdoches except three
Royalist families had fled to Louisiana. It was a
ruse. Toledo, twelve Republican officers, and
about 50 Americans were there intercepting the
fugitives and speeding them on to the Sabine.
Instead of proceeding, Elizondo sent word to all
fugitives that if they presented themselves in Bejar
within fifty days, they would be pardoned. Otherwise, they would be shot.

Twenty-three years later, another army from
the Mexican interior approached San Antonio de
Bejar. Another group of Americans prepared to
hold the city. From the inhabitants they got little
or no cooperation or help. Not knowing about
August of 1813, the Americans branded the San
Antonians as cowards who'd rather live under
tyranny than stand up and fight for freedom.

They'd already stood up and fought for
freedom—and they knew what happened if you
lost. The same man who'd taken great delight in
murdering those who did stand up, in dismember-
ing their corpses, in humiliating and disgracing
their women and starving their children was
commanding the northbound army. People still
lived in San Antonio who had witnessed the dismembered bodies of husbands, brothers, cousins,
or lovers hang from trees and rot for nearly five
years. Girls—women, now—who had ground the
corn for the Spanish army's tortillas by day and
been forced into the soldiers' beds by night, still
remembered. Children, now men and women,
who had been forced to scrounge in garbage heaps
for the fifty-four days Arredondo occupied San
Antonio, remembered. None wanted any part of
another Arredondo vengeance from his favorite
pupil, Santa Anna.

THE MANY FLAGS OF TEXAS

"Six Flags Over Texas" isn't just the name of a theme park between Dallas and Fort Worth, it's a Texas tradition. Students of Texas history, from the very beginning, are drilled on the six national flags that have flown over Texas—the banners of Spain, France, Mexico, the Texas Republic, the Southern Confederacy, and the United States of America. In fact, if we were to say "Sixty Flags Over Texas" we'd probably be closer to right, and in at least two of the six we usually acknowledge we fly the wrong one—sometimes in three. Let's take a look at some of the many, many flags of Texas and see where we're right, wrong, and maybe one way, maybe the other.

There are some very specialized terms used by "vexillologists"—people who study flags (of whom I am not one)—that need to be understood in order to figure out how flags are described. A flag has two basic dimensions: the hoist, which is the vertical measurement, and the fly, which is the horizontal dimension. The usual relationship between hoist and fly is 3:5 a flag is usually three units high (three feet, say) and five units long. Some flags, though, are perfectly square—same dimensions for hoist and fly.

39

The figure in the upper corner of the hoist is called the "union"—the stars are the "union" of the Stars and Stripes. That "union" can be made into a flag in itself, in which case it is called a "jack"— specifically, a union jack. A flag divided into four equal parts is called "quartered." The Spanish Castles and Lions flag is a quartered flag. Now that we've got those terms out of the way, let's look at those Texas flags.

Barring much-earlier incursions by any number of furriners—there are indications that both the Chinese and the Norse, at least, got to Texas before Columbus sailed the ocean blue, though they didn't stay long and didn't, it seems, make too much impression on the locals. Alonzo de Piñeda, a Spanish sea captain who sailed the Texas coast in the early 1500s, was the first outsider to get here, and he flew the Spanish flag. We can say, then, that the Spanish flag was the first flag over Texas— but that was not the castles and lions, made of the quarterings of the coats of arms of Castile and Leon, that is flown as the "Spanish flag" today.

The flag that flew over Texas from the time Piñeda sailed the coast until it was hauled down in 1821—except for a very brief period in the early 1700s—was a white one with a big red-orange X in the middle of it, the ends of the X capped with crowns, with an oval in the middle of the X bearing the coat-of-arms of the Spanish royal family. That "X" is called a "saltire" or a "Cross of St. Andrew." The quarterings—the castles and lions—is a much later flag. It was the saltire that the frontier posts of Spanish Texas flew.

In the late 1600s, as we all know, there was a very brief incursion into Texas by the French, which gave Texas its second flag. René Robert Cavelier, Sieur de La Salle established a settlement he called Fort St. Louis on the Texas coast. What flag flew over it?

About forty years ago, when I was in the fourth grade, at a "Texas History Pageant" staged at Ridgetop School in Austin, the boy representing La Salle and the French walked out on the auditorium stage wearing short pants, tennis shoes with high cardboard swashboot tops, a baggy white shirt, a late-1700s-style tricorne made from his daddy's old hat and decorated with Christmas tinsel and a huge feather—and carrying the red, white, and blue tricolor of France. The tricolor, of course, was the flag of revolutionary France—better than a hundred years after La Salle. Today we're a little more sophisticated; we actually do use the French flags known as "the lilies." We're probably wrong.

There are two "lily" flags: the white one and the blue one. The white banner "seme fleurs de lys or" —with a whole bunch of little-bitty yellow or gold three-pointed flowers on it—was in fact the royal banner of the house of Capet. It was the king of France's personal flag, and it flew only where the king was. Since the king of France certainly never visited the Texas coast, there's very little chance the white-lily banner ever flew over Texas.

The blue banner is dark blue with three or five large gold or yellow fleurs-de-lis. It was the French military flag—flown by the army or the navy. La Salle's expedition was a commercial one, not a military incursion. It wouldn't have flown, then, the military flag. So what flag did La Salle fly?

Frankly, the likelihood is that La Salle didn't have a flag at all. Since La Salle and the captain of the ship that brought him almost wound up killing one another several times, it's very likely that the ship's crew never did give La Salle a flag to fly. If La Salle did have a flag, though, it would most

likely have been the French merchant-marine
ensign. This was a blue flag with a large white
cross on it, the arms of the cross extending from
top to bottom and from end to end of the banner.
Where the arms crossed there was a blue square,
and in that blue square were three small fleurs-de-
lis, which might be white or yellow depending on
who made the flag. If La Salle had a flag, that was
probably the one that flew over Fort St. Louis.

Before the Spanish saltire came down, though,
there was a very important—and almost forgotten—flag that flew over Texas. It came in 1813 with
the abortive revolt called the "Gutiérrez-Magee
Expedition." It was green. That's it—it was solid
green. No figures, no fancy work—just a plain old
green piece of cloth.

The Gutiérrez-Magee flag was the flag of the
first Texas republic, which is, today, sometimes
called the "Green Flag Republic." The standard
history of the revolt is called "Green Flag Over
Texas." Why green?

Perhaps if we were to look at the Americans
who came with Gutiérrez, we might get a better
idea of where that green banner came from. The
two primary American leaders were Augustus
Magee and Samuel Kemper—and both of those
names are Irish as shamrocks. Was the Green Flag
Republic intended to be a new home in the New
World for the persecuted Irish? Unfortunately,
we'll never know, but that's as good an explana-
tion as any that's been offered.

In 1821 Mexico raised its tricolor banner, and
it—except for some minor variations depending on
who made it—hasn't changed much since. It's
divided equally in thirds along the fly, green at the
hoist, white in the center, red on the end. Centered
in the white section is a golden eagle, the national
bird of Mexico, perched on a prickly-pear cactus

and holding a rattlesnake in its beak and one talon. Except for some very minor design changes to that central figure, it's been the same since 1821.

At least two variations of that flag flew in Texas: the state flag of Coahuila y Tejas, which was the green-white-red tricolor with two large "stars" (multipointed sunbursts rather than five- or six-point stars) in black positioned one above the other in the white in place of the eagle and snake; and the "Constitution Flag," which Texicans who supported the Mexican Constitution of 1824 flew as a symbol of their opposition to Santa Anna. It, too, was the tricolor, but with the date 1824 in black centered in the white in place of the eagle and snake.

The Texas Revolution and Republic had its plethora of flags—probably more than at any other time in Texas history. The "Lone Star," as we know it today, wasn't adopted until 1839, and the Texicans who revolted against Mexico had no single flag to follow. At Velasco the Texicans flew, we think—there are contradictory sources—the 1824 flag. Goliad had the "Bloody Arm" flag: a representation of a human arm holding a sword, with blood splashed on the shoulder. Gonzales had the famous "Come and Take it" flag, which wasn't a proper flag at all. It was a big sheet of cloth with a pole at each end, so the Mexican army couldn't accidentally miss the message. It had a picture of the tiny Gonzales cannon painted on it, a black star, and the words "Come and Take it." As we know from history, the Mexican army came—but didn't "take it."

One thing that had arisen from the prerevolutionary upheavals was the concept of the "Lone Star." Texas, against the wishes of those Americans who had become Mexican citizens on the promise that their state would be self-governing, had been combined with Coahuila to make a single state, with the seat of government deep inside Mexico. The flag of Coahuila and Texas had two stars. The Texicans wanted a flag with one star—a separate, self-governing state, and if not a state a republic. The Texicans wanted a Lone Star.

There were at least two very early Lone Star flags: one a white banner with a large blue star in the center and with the words "Liberty or Death" below it, the other a blue banner with a large gold star painted in the center. The big question, though, has always been "Which flag flew over the Alamo?"

Truth told, nobody knows for sure. The only flag known to have survived is the regimental colors of the New Orleans Greys, a blue-grey flag with a spread eagle in black on it, bearing a banner reading "New Orleans Greys." That's the Alamo flag currently on display as a trophy of war in the Chapultepec Castle National Museum in Mexico City. It definitely wasn't, though, "the flag that flew over the Alamo." It wasn't because the Mexican accounts of the battle say "We ripped their banner from the mast." The New Orleans Greys flag was not made with grommets so it could be hoisted and lowered; it was made with a tubelike affair on the hoist so it could be slipped over a pole. That tube is still intact—that flag was never ripped from the mast.

So what flag did fly over the Alamo? At least one somewhat questionable sketch—supposed to have been made during the battle—shows what is unmistakably the two-star tricolor of Coahuila y Tejas. It's sort of unlikely that the Texicans at the Alamo—who were in revolt against the Mexican government partly because Coahuila and Texas had been made into one state and they wanted Texas separate—would fly that flag.

Possibly the most popular "Alamo flag" has been the Constitutional flag—the tricolor with 1824 on it. That flag would have annoyed Santa Anna thoroughly, since he'd deliberately abrogated the Constitution of 1824 to make himself dictator and didn't care to have it thrown back at him. It's also a doubtful flag, though—by the time the Alamo rolled around, Texas was through with any ideas of reconciliation with Mexico under the Constitution of 1824. Those other flags didn't say Liberty Or Death just to have something to say.

There's a very good chance that the flag that flew over the Alamo was brought there by none other than David Crockett himself. Davy had been a soldier, albeit an irregular one, and a congressman. He certainly understood the value of a flag to fight for as a morale booster. On his way to Bexar—present San Antonio—he stopped in East Texas and had a flag made for his Tennessee riflemen to carry. It had thirteen stripes—seven red, six white, with red stripes at the top and bottom. Centered in the flag was a large white star with the letters T-E-X-A-S in black between the points of the star. Thus the Crockett flag combined the thirteen red and white stripes of the flag of the United States— which would have a lot of meaning for the ex-U.S. citizens in the Alamo—with the Lone Star of Texas. That very combination would also be almost sure to infuriate Santa Anna, who considered the United States to be the instigating power behind the Texas revolt anyway.

Simply, though, we don't really know what flag flew over the Alamo. There is some indication that the flag might have survived, at least for a time. An Englishman, writing in 1838, commented that "the colors taken at the Alamo" were on display in the office of the Mexican Ambassador in Belgium. Unfortunately, beyond that he didn't give any indication as to what those "colors" looked like. If we have to pick a flag for the Alamo, what better one to pick than Davy Crockett's?

By the time the battle of San Jacinto rolled around, the Texicans had a flag at last—but not a Lone Star flag. The San Jacinto banner is on display in the Texas State Capitol in Austin, and it's a huge white flag with a picture of a seated woman—whose bodice has slipped, so that things most 19th century ladies preferred to keep covered are hanging out in the breeze—holding a sword. That one we did manage to preserve, but because it wasn't the "Lone Star flag," it never made it as the flag of the Republic.

Texas would have a Lone Star flag—that much was certain. It would also be at least white and blue, preferably red, white and blue. That, too, was certain. What it would look like beyond that remained to be settled.

One of the earliest designs was a very peculiar tricolor—blue on the hoist, white in the middle, red on the fly—in an equally peculiar 1:3 conformation. A flag two feet on the hoist would be six feet on the fly. Centered in the blue section was a single white five-pointed star. This was a very unwieldy flag—much too long to be carried in the normal manner. It seems to have been flown by the Texas navy, but otherwise didn't see much use.

There's very good reason to think that the person who eventually came up with the design for the Lone Star flag was a South Carolinian. South Carolina's state flag, at the time, had a single blue bar 1/3 the length of the flag on the hoist, with white and red bars half the height of the flag on the fly. Centered in the blue bar was a white star. That's exactly the description of Texas' Lone Star flag, but the South Carolina flag's star was much smaller than ours, and in their flag the red bar was on top. The Lone Star flag—the one we have today—was adopted as the flag of the Republic of Texas, became the flag of the state after annexation, and has not been changed since the 1830s. It's one of the oldest "state flags" in the nation and the only "state flag" that was ever the symbol of an independent and sovereign nation (in spite of California's flag with "California Republic" below the bear—the "Bear Flag Republic" lasted a grand total of ten days).

When Anson Jones, last president of the Republic, lowered the Lone Star in Austin, the flagstaff broke and a new one had to be erected to raise the Stars and Stripes. Though the Stars and Stripes was undoubtedly the first United States national flag to be raised over the Texas capitol, it probably wasn't, by any means, the first United States flag to fly on Texas soil. The army came to Texas, and until the 1890s the United States Army, except in wartime, didn't carry the national colors —the Stars and Stripes. Instead, it carried a standard bearing the "Arms of the United States." This was a large blue flag with a golden spread eagle, the one with the shield on his breast, emblazoned on it. It was a national flag of the United States just like the Stars and Stripes, and you saluted it and took your hat off when it passed just like you do today when the Stars and Stripes goes by. The Stars and Stripes was the national "Colors," the "Arms of the United States" was the national "Standard." In addition, any U.S. ships that made harbor in Texas were probably flying the United States Union Jack, which is the blue field with stars that is in the upper hoist of the Stars and Stripes. It can, quite legally, be flown as a separate flag, though it isn't done very often these days. One of the first U.S. flags the new Texians saw, you can bet, was the U.S. Revenue Ensign, which flew on

Revenue Service (now Coast Guard) cutters and over customs houses. It had a blue union with a spread eagle in it, rather than stars, and thirteen red and white stripes running vertically instead of horizontally.

And there things stayed, pretty much, until February of 1861.

Texas was one of the first seven states to secede in 1861, and of them it was the one that had the best reason. While the Radical Republican opposition to slavery was one of the causes Texas cited in its Ordnance of Secession, it also cited the failure or refusal of the United States to live up to the obligations it assumed in the Treaty of Annexation. Specifically, the United States had promised to secure Texas' borders against marauders from Mexico and from other points outside the state. It not only hadn't, it hadn't made much effort to do so. When Texians took matters into their own hands, as when Texas militiamen crossed into the Antelope Hills of Indian Territory to hit raiding Comanches in their home villages, the U.S. government threatened to prosecute the militiamen.

The first new national flag the Confederacy adopted was the Stars and Bars—and it wasn't the "Confederate flag" that you see everywhere these days. That flag, in fact, never existed until the 20th century.

The Stars and Bars had a blue union just like the Stars and Stripes, with seven (later eleven, then thirteen) stars in a circle like on the original Old Glory. It had three stripes—red on top and bottom, white in the middle—each one-third the height of the flag. This flag was the first, and longest-lived, of the three national flags of the Confederacy, and it looked, as you might guess, a lot like the Stars and Stripes, especially at a distance. It was the first Confederate flag to be raised over Texas.

On a hot day at Manassas Junction, Virginia, in the late spring of 1861, Union and Confederate forces met on the battlefield for the first time. (Yankees call it "Bull Run.") At this time a lot of Union units, among them part of the New York state militia, were wearing grey jackets, while a lot of Confederate outfits were still wearing prewar blue coats. General Pierre Gustave Toutant Beauregard was holding his own against a bunch of Yankees but couldn't force forward, and when he spotted a large body of troops marching up on his flank, he was naturally a little concerned about where their sympathies lay. They were wearing blue coats, which didn't necessarily mean Yankee at the battle of First Manassas—Georgia's Clinch Rifles and Louisiana's Washington Artillery, two well-known Confederate outfits, were still wearing blue as late as 1862.

It was a hot, still day, and the bluecoated soldiers' flag hung limply around its pole. It could have been the Stars and Bars—reinforcements— or it could have been the Stars and Stripes, in which case Beauregard was in serious trouble. At a distance, through the gunpowder haze on the battlefield, it was impossible to tell for sure. When at last a stray breeze unfurled the flag and Beauregard could see that it had three stripes rather than thirteen, he no doubt breathed a long sigh of relief—and immediately decided he'd design a more distinctive flag for troops on the battlefield. The result was the Confederate battle flag—the most common, but always unofficial, flag of the Confederacy.

Beauregard's design was a bright red, perfectly square flag—a 1:1 ratio at hoist and fly. It was adorned with a blue saltire or St. Andrew's Cross—

the cross of Scotland's patron saint, and a great
many Southerners were of Scottish descent—out-
lined in white, and had a star in the center of the
cross, with three stars on each arm. While the basic
colors of the flag were red, white, and blue, the
stars could be white, silver, yellow, or gold. Often
the central star was much larger than the others,
and sometimes there was only one star, in the
center. This banner, which is often—and erron-
eously—called "the Stars and Bars" today, was the
soldiers' flag, but it was never the national flag of
the Confederacy. It was always square, by the way,
never oblong like modern "Confederate flags,"
and sometimes it was made with a swallowtail fly,
guidon-style, for cavalry or artillery units.

In 1863 the Confederacy changed its national
flag, and a new flag flew over Texas once again.
Confederate historians call this one, somewhat
romantically, "The Stainless Banner," and it had
its problems. The flag was pure white, made in a
1:2 hoist-to-fly ratio—a flag three feet on the hoist
was six feet, not five, on the fly. In the upper
hoist corner, as a union, was General Beauregard's
battle flag.

It was a beautiful banner, but there was a lot of
white there. If it happened to be hanging limply
on the staff and it hung just right, you couldn't see
the battle flag union. It looked for all the world like
a white flag—a surrender flag.

Well, it wasn't, and it was never intended to be
a surrender flag. Nevertheless, a large number
of Yankees got shot to kittylitter because they
thought the Rebs were surrendering—they were,
after all, flying a white flag—when in fact the Rebs
were charging. This, the Confederacy decided, was
downright unchivalrous. A feller ought to fight
under a flag that nobody could mistake for a surrender flag. This is the flag, by the way, that was

the legal national flag of the Confederacy and therefore of Texas when Dick Dowling and his 47 Irishmen routed a Yankee fleet, sunk two gunboats and a transport, and captured 3000 muskets and accoutrement sets and 1200 Yankee soldiers, including a general officer, at Sabine Pass.

In 1864 the Confederacy—and consequently Texas—got a new national flag. It was simply a modification of the Stainless Banner, but the flag's dimensions were set at a more normal 3:5 ratio, and a bright red vertical bar 1/4 the length of the flag was added to the end of the fly. While this was, until June of 1865, when Texas finally surrendered after winning the last land battle of the war at Palmito Ranch, the official national flag of the nation in which Texas was a state, it probably never got to Texas and may never have flown here. Nonetheless, it is quite legally a "flag of Texas."

The United States brought the Stars and Stripes back in 1865, but it's entirely likely the flag which flew over the state capitol didn't necessarily look much like what we'd recognize as the Stars and Stripes today. There were no official rules as to how the Stars and Stripes was to look until the 1890s. It was legal for the stars to have five, six, or even seven points, and for them to be silver or gold instead of white. There were no rules about how the stars were arranged in the union, either—the only statement was that they should represent "a new constellation." Stars were arranged in concentric circles, in irregular rows, in various patterns limited only by the imagination and sewing skill of the flagmaker. Only the stripes— thirteen in number, seven red, six white—with a blue union containing the stars were specified.

The Stars and Stripes has flown over the Texas capitol—alongside the Lone Star—since June of 1865. The only suggestion of change came in the

1940s, when Texas governor W. Lee O'Daniel appointed himself senator to fill the unexpired term left by the death of one of Texas' senators. O'Daniel became governor on the basis of his recognition from radio, where he had been sales manager—and radio voice—of the Burrus Mills of Corsicana, Texas, selling Light Crust Flour with country fiddling, generated by the Lightcrust Dough Boys: guitarist Herman Arnspiger and a couple of fiddlers named Jim Bob and Johnny Lee Wills.

O'Daniel was something of a joke to the rest of the country—a jumped-up biscuit salesman who thought he could "show 'em how to do it right" in national politics—and O'Daniel's attitudes and antics as senator did little to change this impression. A suggestion was made in the United States Congress—perhaps only half as a joke—that the blue union of the Stars and Stripes be altered to contain, instead of 48 stars, 47 stars and a circle. Forty-seven stars and a biscuit.

THE COUNTERREVOLUTION
OF 1838-1840

Let's step back in time to the evening of April 21, 1836. Sion Bostick and his four pals have hauled in the well-dressed private they caught hiding in the tules in his underdrawers, and he's been identified by his own men as "El Presidente"—Excelencio Antonio López de Santa Anna y Pérez de LeBrón, Presidente de la Republica y Comandante del Ejercitio de Mejico. Every piece of rope over ten feet long within five miles or so of San Jacinto has a hangman's knot in it, and fellers are odd-manning for the privilege and honor of whipping the horse out from under "ol' Santy Anner." The lady who owns the ground on which the battle was fought has told Sam Houston, in colorful and certain terms, to get all the carcasses out of her pasture before they stink the place up. Dr. Labadie has done what he can to bandage Sam's foot, and Santa Anna has bitten his lip and congratulated Houston on capturing "The Napoleon of the West."

Now Sam has a problem—what'll he do with Santa Anna? The army—and most of the rest of Texas—wants to see him swing from a cottonwood limb. Houston stands almost alone in understanding just how dumb that could be. "Santa Anna alive," he tells Texas, "is the President of Mexico, and we've got him. Santa Anna dead is just another dead Mexican soldier."

Well, there was a mite more to it than just that. Santa Anna alive was in the situation of a small, loudmouthed bully whose entourage of big, mean followers suddenly disappears, who finds himself inescapably in the clutches of the very folks he's been bullying—and they're fightin' mad. He was scared out of his fancy silk underpants.

Houston realized that if Texas executed Santa Anna, regardless of evidence—the Goliad Massacre would do for starters—that indicated if anyone ever should be a cottonwood blossom it was the small, extremely frightened "Napoleon of the West," Mexico would regard the execution as a mortal insult. Texas won San Jacinto by a fluke, and nobody knew that better than Sam. Had the Mexican army been ready for battle instead of being taken by surprise, it would have eaten the small, undisciplined rabble Houston called the "Texas army" for lunch and gone looking for dessert afterwards.

The execution of Santa Anna would probably unite all of Mexico—including those Mexicans, of whom there were many, who hated Santa Anna's guts and would cheerfully hang him themselves if they got the chance—in a war of national vengeance against the exhausted, disorganized, undisciplined, and underarmed Texicans. That would be a war the fledgling Republic of Texas could not hope to win, even by accident.

On the other hand, with Santa Anna alive at Houston's sufferance and with the shadow of a hangman's noose clearly visible on his prison wall, the dictator would agree to anything— probably including kissing the feet of every surviving Texican and going on his hands and knees while rolling a peanut with his nose all the way back to the Rio Grande—that would keep that ominous rope-shadow on the wall empty and the rope itself off his neck. Houston understood that and knew Texas could extort—there's really no other way to describe negotiations that begin with "sign or hang"—a very favorable treaty out of the dictator. That is exactly what Sam Houston proceeded to do.

In the treaty Santa Anna agreed that Texas owned not merely the land the Anglo-Americans actually controlled, but all the rest of present-day Texas, better than half of New Mexico, about a third of Colorado, and bits and pieces of Oklahoma and Wyoming. This included Mexico's major northern trade outlet, Santa Fe, and—if Texas could make it stick—would turn the very lucrative Santa Fe trade with the U.S. over to Texas, as well as a substantial silver- and gold-mining area in New Mexico and Colorado. Texas would need that gold and silver if it was to survive as a nation.

In fact, the actual boundary of the Republic of Texas—as opposed to the treaty boundary—was pretty much one good rifle-shot beyond the west bank of the Nueces, not the Rio Grande. Mexican troops continued to occupy the border towns on both sides of the Rio Bravo (as Mexico, even today, calls what we call the Rio Grande), and it's for dead sure that the prosperous traders of Santa Fe never considered themselves citizens of the Republic of Texas. In fact, the few expeditions Texians—as they were beginning to call themselves—mounted to assert their treaty-recognized right of possession to the land beyond the Nueces came to disaster.

Santa Anna, after signing the treaty, was finally allowed to go home. He had been humiliated—

forced not merely to sign a treaty that gave away much of Mexico, but personally humiliated as well. At one point he was so terrified of being hanged that he embraced Houston, cried into the lapels of the big man's coat like a frightened child, and begged his conqueror not to let him be hanged. Santa Anna, at least in his own eyes, was still "The Napoleon of the West," and he could not suffer those who had so thoroughly humiliated him—even if they did spare his life—to survive and tell the world of his humiliation. Texas had to be reconquered and the insulting personal humiliation erased—and no sooner had Santa Anna reached home than he (and, of course, the Mexican Congress, which was and had been all along in Santa Anna's pocket—mostly because he'd hanged or shot any member who wasn't) repudiated the treaty in its entirety and began to plan to reconquer the lost territory and punish the upstart "norteños."

There was something going on in the "old States" that would profoundly influence what would happen in Texas for the next few years. In northern Georgia and Alabama lived the most civilized of the "Five Civilized Tribes"—the Cherokees. Cherokees had "walked the white man's road" more thoroughly than any other tribe. They became farmers, planters, and merchants in what was known as "the Nickajack country"—northern Georgia and Alabama—and they prospered. Cherokee children went to school, Cherokee families and long-resident white families intermarried. Cherokees were slave-owners (though they had, to their white neighbors' way of thinking, a distressing habit of marrying their slave women and freeing them and the offspring of the unions), and, all in all, Cherokees were well on the way to becoming an important and prosperous part of society in the region.

Into the Nickajack moved land-hungry whites from the states to the north—and there were a bunch of Injuns squatting on land white folks might be farming. Never mind that these "Injuns" were slaveholders who plowed ground and planted cash crops, lived in fine two-story white houses, rode in two-horse carriages, and wore clawhammer coats and stiff collars on Sunday— they were still "Injuns." To the new arrivals that made 'em bad, and they began to agitate to remove the Cherokees to a "reservation" somewhere to the west. Stories began to circulate of "Injun atrocities," and nightriders began to ride. Shots were exchanged, and not all those who fell before them were Indians. An "Indian uprising"—which never actually existed—was manufactured, and the president of the United States, Andrew Jackson, ordered the expulsion of the Cherokees from Alabama and Georgia to the ill-defined "Indian territory" that would someday be Oklahoma. Officially, it's called "The Cherokee Removal." To the Cherokees, it has another name—"The Trail Of Tears."

Some of those Cherokees, under a chief called The Bowl (sometimes mistakenly called "Chief Bowls" or "Chief Bowles"), remembered that the Cherokees' long-time white-man friend, Sam Houston, whom the Cherokees named "The Raven," once senator from Tennessee and later governor of that state, who'd often championed the cause of the Cherokees in Congress, was now a big chief in a place called Texas, somewhere out where the Trail of Tears ended. The Bowl and his people headed for wherever The Raven lighted. (There is, just for the record, a rumor that holds that the name the Cherokees gave Houston was not "The Raven" but "The Raving," as in "The Raving Drunk," but that's not part of this story.)

Houston was delighted to have his old friends and allies in his new country. He helped settle The Bowl and his people to the north of the main white settlements, intending to make of the Cherokees—and any other allied tribes he could attract to Texas—a buffer between the struggling heartland of Texas to the south and east and the wild "blanket Indians" like the Comanches and Kiowas to the north and west. Besides being "civilized" in the white-man sense and industrious farmers, the Cherokees had been—and could be again, if reason for it arose—a nation of powerful warriors. Houston could see—and he assumed anyone else of vision could see—the advantage of having a buffer of a powerful group of warrior-farmers between the wild raiders of the north and west and the farms and plantations of the Anglo-Texians. In order to get to the Anglos, the Comanches would have to come through the Cherokees, and that just might, in the old frontier expression, take 'em a mite longer'n they figgered.

Unfortunately for The Bowl and his people, the new republic's constitution mandated a two-year term for the "Big Chief"—the president—and by law the president of Texas could not succeed himself. The second president of the Republic was Mirabeau Bounaparte Lamar, who'd risen from corporal to colonel of cavalry on the field of battle at San Jacinto and been promoted for outstanding courage and gallantry in direct contact with the enemy. Lamar was from Alabama and he hated Indians—all Indians, but particularly Cherokees. (Just incidentally, Lamar was also a fiscal incompetent who destroyed Texas' credit and probably did more to guarantee that the Republic of Texas would eventually join the United States than any other single figure in Republic of Texas history. That, however, isn't part of this story. No more than is the fact that, as a former schoolteacher, he realized the value of education and conceived the idea of a national university system for the Republic, setting aside public land for the support of such a system, which eventually became the nucleus of The University of Texas. It took as its motto Lamar's dictum "A cultivated mind is the guardian of democracy," the Latinized version of which is Disciplina Praesidium Civitatis. You'll find it cut in stone on the UT tower in Austin.)

Santa Anna, in the meantime, was having troubles of his own. He had to silence as quickly as possible any and all potential revolts against his regime—which, of course, meant he had to shoot a lot of people. He'd also managed to default on some loans from France, and some French warships sailed into Vera Cruz, seized the customshouse, and applied the customs-duties of Mexico to the payment of the loans until they were satisfied. This was embarrassing, and he had to shoot some more people to cover his embarrassment. What with one thing and another, it was 1837 before he could turn his attention to the reconquest of Texas.

As early as 1836 rumors had been circulating that Mexican agents were busy among Texas Indians, trying to stir up trouble for the Texas Republic. On April 12, even before San Jacinto, a man named Miguel de Cortinez testified to Major General Edmund P. Gaines, the U.S. Army officer in command at Natchitoches, Louisiana, that Miguel's brother Eusebio had been commissioned by Mexican General Martín Perfectó de Cós to agitate Indians in the old Neutral Strip that separated Texas and Louisiana against the Anglo Texans. A little later Lieutenant Joseph Bonnell told General Gaines that a couple of Mexican agents named Manuel Flores and Jose Maria Medrano were in Louisiana trying to stir up trouble with the Indians. All of this prompted Gaines to move to the Sabine with a strong force just in case Indians from U.S. territory decided to get into the fight. Nothing happened.

In the summer of 1837 a delegation of Cherokees actually went to Matamoros, and a plan was laid whereby the Indians would assemble between San Antonio and Nacogdoches. As soon as they were ready, General Vicente Filisola and 5000 men would cross the Rio Grande and drive east while the Indians attacked westward. The Cherokees were to receive "guaranteed possession of their hunting grounds in Texas" and were to form a buffer between Mexico and the United States. Nothing came of this, either.

According to accepted "history," all Texans were enthusiastic over the new Republic, but that's nowhere near true. In fact a great many people, not just Hispanics but North American and European Texas settlers as well, were not at all happy with the way things were shaping up in the new Republic. The hotbed of this anti-Republic sentiment was the old Spanish/Mexican town founded by Gil Ybarbo, Nacogdoches. The ringleaders were Vincente Cordova and Nathaniel Norris.

On May 29, 1838, a force of about 120 men—recorded as "72 citizens, 2 Indians, 34 soldiers from La Bahia, and 20 Cherokee and Caddo Indians"—left Matamoros under the command of Pedro Julian Miracle and crossed the Rio Grande into country that, by treaty, belonged to the Republic of Texas. On August 20, 1838, at the junction of Caney Creek and the Red River, Miracle was killed—most likely murdered—and his body searched. In his possession was a diary detailing the progress of his expedition from the time it entered Texas to the day he died. It told of visits to the Choctaw, Cherokee, Kickapoo, Keechi, Chickasaw, Caddo, Waco, and Tawakoni Indians, and to Cordova and Norris in Nacogdoches. On July 19 of the same year, Cordova wrote to General Manuel Flores in Mexico, telling Flores that Cordova had been commissioned by General Filisola to recruit Indians as allies to the Mexican army, and that he had actually begun recruiting among the Cherokees.

On August 7, 1838, Captain John Durst of the Texas Militia reported to his commander, Major General Thomas J. Rusk, that Cordova and Norris, together with a party of 100 or more armed men and some Indian allies, were camped on the Angelina River. The information was passed to Sam Houston, who—as president—proclaimed the group "enemies of the Republic" and ordered them to go home. Instead they sent Houston a list of grievances and demands and stayed where they were. By August 10 Cordova and Norris had something like 450 men—about 150 discontented Mexicans and other colonists and 300 or so Indians of various tribes. The group then began to move north.

General Thomas J. Rusk was sure that Cordova intended to go recruit the Cherokees of The Bowl. Rusk headed directly for The Bowl's village, sending Major Henry W. Augustine to follow Cordova and keep an eye on him. Very shortly Augustine reported that Cordova was not headed for the Cherokees at all—he had changed directions and was going toward the Kickapoo village on the upper Trinity. Rusk immediately moved to attack the Kickapoo village, but the Indians met him on the way. The Indians lost 11 killed, Rusk had 11 wounded. Cordova continued to march and countermarch around the northeast portion of the Republic for the remainder of 1838, keeping Rusk and his men busy.

In February of 1839 General Valentin Canalizo replaced Filisola in command of the Mexican north, and he immediately issued orders to the agents among the Indians. The Mexicans, he said, were having too much trouble with the French to invade Texas at the moment, but the agents were to get the Indians to stir up as much trouble as possible. The Indian allies were to occupy, if possible, a line from San Antonio to the Guadalupe and from the Leon to the mouth of the San Marcos. This would put their Mexican allies behind them and the Anglo-Texians in front, and then they were to burn houses and fields and harrass the Anglos any way they could.

In March Cordova and a group of 64, including Anglos, Mexicans, Indians, and runaway slaves, started for Matamoros to discuss detailed plans with Canalizo. They tried to avoid all contact with and detection by the Anglo-Texians, but two seasoned frontiersmen, George W. Davis and Reuben Hornsby, picked up their trail near Waterloo (part of Austin, today) and gave the alarm.

On March 27 Colonel Edward Burleson heard of a large group of "Indians" camped "at the foot of the mountains on the Colorado" (in the vicinity of present Marshall Ford Dam in Austin, close to where Bee Cave Road crosses the Colorado) and raised a force of 79 volunteers to deal with the problem. Burleson's scouts reported that the "Indians" had crossed the Colorado and were headed toward Seguin. Very shortly afterwards, some ten miles southwest of Waterloo, Burleson got word that another trail of a large party of Indians had been spotted near Waterloo, and the volunteers turned back to deal with the more immediate problem. It turned out to be part of the trail they were already following, so—having lost about 20 miles of travel—Burleson and 75 of his original 79 headed back for Seguin.

The Burleson party made their camp on Bear Creek, southwest of Austin, and met a man named Robinson. He'd been with Cordova but deserted, and he told Burleson that the party was not Indians at all, but Vicente Cordova and his followers. He also told the Texians that Cordova was headed to Mexico to get guns and ammunition for the Indians, after which he would direct a guerrilla war against the Anglo settlements.

On the 28th Burleson's scouts located the Cordova party, which was camped on Mill Creek near the Guadalupe (just north of the Battleground Prairie historical marker on U.S. 90A east of Seguin). Burleson immediately divided his men and placed his right wing under Captain Micah Andrews, while Captain Jesse Billingsley got the left. Burleson then ordered the Texians to charge the Cordova group, which was caught completely off guard.

The books describe what happened as "a running battle," but most of the shooting was being done by the Texians. It was, in fact, an out-and-out rout. The Texian forces chased Cordova's fleeing men for about five miles, shooting all the while, and apparently little return fire was offered. Estimates of casualties differ. Burleson reported killing 30 and wounding "many," including Cordova, as well as capturing 19. Other sources claim only 18 or 19 killed. Though Burleson reported no Texian casualties, other sources say three were wounded and none killed. Cordova himself escaped and reached Mexico, though his wound was apparently a severe one and he never returned to Texas.

The name Manuel Flores bounces in and out of
the Republic's history a dozen times or more
between 1835 and 1839. Exactly who—or, more to
the point, what—Flores was remains a matter of
conjecture on this side of the Rio Grande.

We know that following the Cordova-Norris
fight at Battleground Prairie east of Seguin, the
Texians were awake to the possibility, even the
likelihood, that there would be more attempts at
invasion and more attempts to stir up the Indians
on behalf of Mexico. Captives taken at the Mill
Creek fight told the Texians that Cordova intended
to return to Texas shortly, and he would be bringing guns, powder, lead, and flints to the Indians,
as well as presents and perhaps gold—the
Cherokees, for one group, certainly understood
gold. A "ranging company" of twenty men under
Captain Micah Andrews was given the task of
patrolling the western edge of the settlements,
protecting the settlers from—or at least warning
them of—Indian attacks, and keeping a weather
eye out for further Mexican forays.

Sometime in May of 1839 Manuel Flores, called
"General Flores" in many histories, though his
actual military capacity seems to be doubtful,
began a trip to visit the "Northern Indians" in
Texas. He may have been the same "General
Manuel Flores" to whom Cordova wrote and the
same Manuel Flores Lieutenant Bonnell reported
as being in Louisiana before San Jacinto, but both
the Christian name Manuel and the surname
Flores are extremely common. The Flores party
included Ensign Juan de la Garza, thirteen
Mexicans (mostly soldiers), eleven Indians, and
over 100 head of horses and pack animals laden
with about 300 pounds each of gunpowder and
lead, together with other plunder. (The rank
ensign is equivalent to today's second lieutenant.)

De la Garza, not Flores, held a special commission from General Valentin Canalizo to enlist as many Texas Indians as possible on the side of the Mexican government. This does tend to throw some doubt upon the almost universally applied title "general" for this particular Manuel Flores.

We don't know for sure when or where Flores entered Texas or how long he'd been here before May 14, 1839, but on that date, between San Antonio de Bejar and Seguin, the Mexican party was surprised to run head-on into a party of Texas surveyors. The official report says they "murdered" the surveyors and they did in fact kill them, but it seems likely there was a fight of some sort involved. The surveyors were not the entire party, and the remainder heard the gunfire. They investigated, saw the Mexican party and their dead companions, and immediately reported to Colonel Burleson. Burleson got some volunteers together and set out in pursuit, but the trail was cold and Flores was moving fairly fast.

They were tracked to a crossing on the Guadelupe at present-day New Braunfels, from where they headed in the general direction of Waterloo (Austin). Late on the 15th they were spotted by two of Captain Andrews' foragers, who were out hunting venison for supper. The Texians reported that they had seen a large number of horses and/or mules, but because of the lateness, the poor light, and the distance involved, they were unable to determine if the animals were ridden or simply a band of wild horses. Andrews determined to investigate and find out and, after several hours of hard riding, caught up with the tail-end of Flores' column as it entered a dense cedarbreak on the afternoon of the 16th.

The hunters reported a "large number" of horses and mules. Andrews and his men saw only the rear of the column as it disappeared into the cedarbreak. The twenty Texians had no idea how many more Mexicans and/or Indians might be waiting inside the thicket, ready to fire from concealment or to ambush their party. They closed to within fifty yards, close enough to determine that they were, in fact, dealing with a column of Mexicans in a place where it had no business, and then retired to get reinforcements.

A lot of the "ranging company" disagreed with the retirement. They insisted that the party was not, after all, a large one, and if they attacked the column—especially when it was moving and away from cover or when it was camped—they could win a fight with it. Andrews eventually agreed and the Texians resumed the pursuit. The next day Andrews' horse came up lame, as did at least three others during the chase, and the pursuing party wound up with seventeen men under Lieutenant James O. Rice.

On the morning of the 18th Rice and his men found where Flores' command camped on the South San Gabriel River near present-day Liberty Hill. They apparently decided they'd lost or scared off their pursuers, for they'd cut down a bee-tree for honey near where they camped. Shortly afterwards the Texians again came up on the end of the Flores column, and this time they attacked. The historical marker which sits alongside a county road just north of Texas 29, a little east of the community of Seward's Junction where 29 crosses U.S. 183, marks fairly well the beginning of the pursuit.

Williamson County Road 266 crosses the South San Gabriel River at this ford, which was in use by Indians when white men first came to the limestone hills. The general description of Manuel Flores' route northward points to use of this ford. His last campsite was probably within 100 yards of this site.

(Williamson Co. Rd 266 leads south from Texas 29 approximately 1.7 miles east of the junction of Texas 29 and US 183.)

It was another chase. The Texians recorded that the enemy attempted to make a stand and give them a battle several times, but the Texas forces continued to push them hard, giving them no chance to get set. The pursuit continued for about seven or eight miles to the east, finally ending on a hogback ridge overlooking the North San Gabriel River. The hogback, just incidentally, is just across the east fence of the old Fred Eckhardt place in west-central Williamson County, on property formerly owned by Dr. John Nichols.

There the Flores party finally did make its only stand, and the Texians promptly killed Flores and two more of his men. Those who survived fled toward the Brazos, leaving all their plunder behind.

In addition to powder and lead and "one hundred fourteen horses and mules and all their packing apparatus," the Texians found some very interesting papers on Flores' body. One was a letter from General Canalizo addressed to the chiefs of the Caddos, Seminoles, Kickapoos, and Cherokees, urging them to follow Flores and to join up with Mexico, and especially not to expect anything from the Texians, who he said were "greedy adventurers for land, who wish to deprive you even of the sun which warms and vivifies you, and who will not cease to injure you while the grass grows and the water flows."

Flores was also carrying a letter from Cordova addressed to those of his followers who had stayed behind, telling them that he wouldn't be coming back to Texas "at present" because he was wounded. This was the first confirmation the Texians had that Cordova had been wounded near Seguin on March 28.

IN THIS VICINITY

MANUEL FLORES

AN EMISSARY OF THE MEXICAN
GOVERNMENT, WITH A SMALL GROUP
OF MEN CONVEYING AMMUNITION
TO THE INDIANS ON THE LAMPASAS
RIVER, WAS SURPRISED BY RANGERS
UNDER LIEUTENANT J. O. RICE IN
MAY, 1839, AND KILLED

The Manuel Flores monument, today, stands at the junction of Texas 29 and Williamson County Road 260 on the north side of 29 approximately 1.7 miles east of the junction of 29 and US 183, called "Seward's Junction." It formerly stood alongside the county road about 3/4 mile northeast of this site. At that time, it was very close to the spot where Rice's rangers began their shooting pursuit.

That's the history. Where history ends, legend takes over. Texas historian J. Frank Dobie, in a section of his book *Coronado's Children* entitled "Steinheimer's Millions," tells us that a German named Steinheimer was with Flores for much of his travels, quitting only hours before the Texians caught up. Steinheimer, says Dobie, had grown rich in mining in Mexico and was enroute to the United States with a great load of gold bullion and gold nuggets. He turned north as Flores turned east, was later ambushed by Indians, and was forced to bury his fortune among "a bunch of knobs on the prairie." He allegedly left a map, which found its way to a former sweetheart in St. Louis. People have been digging holes in everything that looks like "a bunch of knobs on the prairie" in the hundred miles or so to the north and east of Liberty Hill ever since.

In my childhood we had another maybe so/ maybe not treasure story associated with Manuel Flores. One thing the Texians did not find, either on Flores' body or on the pack animals, was anything that looked like money. But why not? The Cherokees certainly understood what money was and how it could be used, and so did the Caddos. The Kickapoos and Seminoles had been around white men long enough to understand the value of coins—they weren't about to be bought with a bunch of looking glasses and colored beads. Where, folks wondered, was the money Flores had to be carrying?

Local tradition provided at least a part of a possible answer. Amiel Ischy, who'd lived in the country all his life and whose family had lived there for a hundred years or so when I knew him, was told as a child that "them Mexicans, they throwed somethin-nother down one a them sink-holes on top a that hogback, an' then they throwed some dynamite in there with it." He also found, years before, a huge rock with a "map of Texas," and "F 40" painted on it, which his grandfather told him was left by the Texians as a marker "where they killed ol' Flores an' his forty Mexicans."

Tradition holds that in this immediate vicinity J. O. Rice and his rangers ran Manuel Flores and the survivors of the eight-mile chase to ground. Tradition also holds that Rice (or someone) marked the spot by painting "a map of Texas" and "F 40" (supposedly for "Flores and his forty Mexicans") on a large flat rock near here. On this ridge is a limestone sinkhole, one of many in the area, which may be the one into which Flores' men dropped "something" and followed it with an explosive charge. When the hole, now choked with debris, was open, the author found nothing but limestone and a previously uncatalogued cave-dwelling lizard inside. (Location on private property nine miles west of the San Gabriel bridge on Texas 29 and approximately three miles north of the highway. Not accessible to public.)

Leaving out the dynamite—it wasn't invented until 1866—and the "forty Mexicans"—the actual count was 24, 11 of those were Indians, and the Texians only killed three, Flores and two others—this legend might have a grain of truth in it. If Flores' men did throw "somethin-nother" down a sinkhole and drop an explosive charge of some sort in with it, what would they have been likely to be hiding in such a manner?

What didn't the Texians find on Flores or on his pack animals that his mission almost surely dictated he would be carrying? Money—in some form or another, most likely in gold coin or bullion. Not much to go on, to be sure, but a lot of folks (and I don't blush a bit when I admit I was one of them for quite a while) have spent a lot of time digging on that hogback.

THE EXPULSION OF THE CHEROKEES

Perhaps the single most shameful—and downright foolish, to boot—thing done by Texians under the Republic was the removal of the Cherokees. Still, considering the circumstances— the Cherokees, like many other tribes, had in fact been in some sort of contact with the Mexican government, and Cherokees representing the villages in Northeast Texas had in fact attended a council in Matamoros, and considering all other conditions existing in 1839, what the Texians did, while certainly not "honorable" and probably not justified, is understandable in terms of the times. What the United States did in 1942, in exiling Japanese-Americans from their west coast homes to what were, in effect, concentration camps in a desert, was neither "honorable" nor justified—we know that through hindsight—but, given the conditions as they existed in the immediate wake of Pearl Harbor, it was and is understandable.

What the Texians did was, mostly, just plain stupid—and they paid for it over the years. Not in cash, and not to the Cherokees, but in their own blood, spilled in raids by the "blanket Indians" from the north. Raids the Cherokees might have absorbed or fought off, had they been let be.

Mirabeau Bounaparte Lamar had no sooner taken office as president of the Republic of Texas than he began moves to oust the Cherokees and all other Indians—except of course the Comanches, Apaches, and the like, who weren't "oustable" at the moment. Shortly after his inauguration he signed a bill providing for a regiment of 840 men, to be enlisted for three years. These men were supposed to "patrol and protect the frontiers," but their actual purpose was to run as many Indians as possible out of Texas. He also demanded that a military road be built, from the Kiamisha Red River to the Nueces, and a line of forts constructed along it. Very shortly afterwards, he authorized the calling for eight companies of mounted volunteers—"ranging companies"—to serve for six months at a time as needed.

The Cherokees felt they were secure in their land, at least. In a treaty signed with the provisional government even before Texas declared its independence—on February 20, 1836, in fact—the Cherokees were granted legal title to their lands. Lamar said that the treaty was "a nullity when made—is inoperative now—has never been sanctioned by this Government and never will be." He insisted that the Cherokees had come to Texas on their own and settled on lands to which they had no title, but were allowed to remain by the Republic as long as they obeyed the laws of the Republic and didn't make attacks upon settlers who were "legitimate." He also insisted that the evidence "convicted" the Cherokees of conspiring with Mexico and other Indian tribes to violate the laws and attack the citizens of Texas. He then sent a letter to The Bowl, telling him that the Republic's government was fully aware of all the Cherokees' dealings with not just Mexico but with Cordova as well, and telling The Bowl that Texas hoped to achieve a "peaceful removal" of the Cherokees to somewhere outside the Republic's boundaries, since their presence could no longer be tolerated. Lamar also sent Major B. C. Waters with some volunteers to the "great saline"—a huge salt-lick near the present town of Grand Saline—to build a fort.

This was Cherokee land and The Bowl knew it. He met Waters with a force of warriors and told him, in no uncertain terms, to go back where he came from or he'd wish he had. Waters left.

Lamar, understandably, didn't like that, but he didn't have near as many soldiers handy as The Bowl had warriors. He sent The Bowl another letter, claiming that the fort was being built only for the purpose of preventing hostile Indians and various Mexican agents from coming into Cherokee country, was solely for the protection of Texas settlers, and wasn't intended to harass the Cherokees. To which The Bowl undoubtedly said the Cherokee equivalent of "Yeah—sure." Or words to that effect.

The Bowl, by this time, was disgusted with the whole business. He agreed that the Indian and the white man—at least his Indians and these particular white men—would never be able to live side by side in peace. He sent word to Lamar that the Cherokees would leave Texas peaceably—if they were paid for the improvements on their land. Lamar at least claimed to accept the terms and appointed a commission of five men—David G. Burnet, James S. Mayfield, Thomas J. Rusk, Albert Sidney Johnston, and I. W. Barton—to discuss terms with The Bowl and his people. It's interesting to note that at least three of these men—Burnet, Rusk, and Johnston—agreed whole-heartedly with Lamar that "the only good Injun's a dead Injun and the sooner he gets that way the better." Since Lamar also appointed Mayfield and Barton, we can probably conclude they felt the same way. The cards were stacked against The Bowl and his people, no matter what happened next.

According to the commission's report—and that's all we have to go on—the commission worked for several days trying to reach a settlement with The Bowl and the Cherokees, offering to have the improvements on Cherokee land fairly appraised and to pay the Cherokees "in silver and goods" for those improvements before the Indians left. Who was to do the appraising the commission doesn't say, nor did it ever say where Texas—which was already nearly broke and going broker by the day—was going to get the "silver and goods" to pay off the Indians. On July 15 the commission announced that negotiations had failed.

Lamar had apparently been expecting the negotiations to fail, because in the meantime he'd moved about 900 men—soldiers and volunteers—into the Cherokees' country. On the very day the commission broke off negotiations, the army began its march on the villages from close by. The troops were under the overall command of Brigadier General Kelsey H. Douglass, with the ubiquitous Edward Burleson, Major W. J. Jones, and Colonel Willis H. Landrum commanding sections. Landrum immediately crossed the Neches River and marched up the west bank to cut off any retreat or reinforcements, while Burleson—who'd been joined by Lieutenant General Rusk (one of the commission, please note) and Lieutenant Colonel Deveraux J. Woodlief—went charging into the main village of the Cherokees, only to find it abandoned.

The Bowl had pulled his men back to a ravine and dense woods near a Delaware village, and as soon as the troops pushed into range, the Cherokees opened fire. An attack was made, personally led by Burleson, Rusk, and Woodlief, which chased the Indians out of their position. The Texas forces lost two killed, six wounded (one died later), and the official report says that eighteen Cherokee corpses were found on the field. The Texians reported capturing "five kegs of powder, 250 lbs lead, many horses, and cattle, corn, and other property." This included most of the Cherokees' personal belongings as well.

The next morning the troops began to pursue the Cherokees in earnest, and it didn't take long to catch up with them. The Indians had somewhere between 400 and 500 warriors, plus women and children to protect, and the Texians had about 900 troops—and no women and children to worry about. A short but violent battle was fought in a cornfield, and the Indians retreated into a thicket. Another short battle forced them to pull back into the swamps along the Neches bottom, and there the Texians charged them. In a battle that lasted about an hour and a half, the Indians lost nearly one man out of four, either killed or wounded. The Texians lost two killed and thirty wounded (three died later). Among those wounded were David G. Burnet, then vice-president of the Republic, the Republic's adjutant general, Hugh McLeod, General Albert Sidney Johnston, and Major David S. Kaufman. (Nobody ever said these guys were cowards, folks—dumb, maybe, but never cowardly.)

On the Indian side, The Bowl—who was the only real leader the Cherokees had at the time—was killed. Legend holds that the sword he wore on the battlefield—which was stolen from his body—was one captured on the San Jacinto battlefield and presented to The Bowl by Houston. It also holds that the man who killed and scalped The Bowl also peeled strips of skin off the old man's back, tanned them, and later plaited them into a quirt. And if you go up to the Neches bottoms today, you can find a lady who insists that The Bowl is still there—walking under the elms where he fought his last fight.

For the next several days the Texians rampaged through the Indian villages of the area, capturing and scattering livestock and burning houses and crops. General Douglass saw, among the other Indians in the area—the Delawares, Shawnees, Caddos, Kickapoos, Biloxis, Creeks, Weechees, Muskogees, and Seminoles—what he claimed were fields of corn, beans, and peas sufficient to support at least a thousand Indians, plus the entire Mexican army, for a year. He burned much of this food in the field and recommended that the rest be burned as soon as possible. Considering that the Indians planted food for an entire year at a time and didn't trade for or buy it, Douglass' estimate of the number the Indians intended to feed was probably excessive.

The troops continued to chase the Cherokees until the 25th, by which time most of them had fled to Arkansas and what is now Eastern Oklahoma. The chieftainship passed to John Bowl, The Bowl's son, and to another man named The Egg. These two leaders and a small portion of the band remained hiding on the upper Trinity until winter, when they and a small remnant tried to get to Mexico. On Christmas Day, 1839, Burleson and his ranging company caught up with them on the San Saba River. In the fight both John Bowl and The Egg, as well as five more Cherokee men, were killed. Burleson captured twenty-seven women and children including The Bowl's wife, John Bowl's wife and two children, and John Bowl's two sisters. The Texians took all the Cherokees' horses and gear, as well as some cattle they were taking along. The Texians lost two men—Captain John J. Lynch and a Tonkawa Indian tracker. The Cherokees who escaped eventually found their way to Oklahoma, but the expulsion of the Cherokees was complete.

In a way, Lamar's expulsion of the Cherokees was a success. The more settled areas east of the Brazos were seldom bothered by Indians after this—but the frontier was left wide open for the Comanches, Kiowas, and Apaches.

THE COUNCIL HOUSE FIGHT

Compared to the Comanches, the Cherokees were a bunch of prank-loving kids. Though Lamar made a big thing about chasing out the Cherokees and the other Indian tribes in East Texas, Lewis P. Cooke, on March 12, 1839, wrote to General Albert Sidney Johnston "the whole country (west of the lower Colorado and upper Brazos) is literally swarming with redskins" and insisted that if some relief were not given the frontier settlers, they would have to abandon the entire area to the Indians. While the rhetoric was somewhat flamboyant, it was a fair statement of the case. The Comanches raided pretty much when and where they pleased just about anywhere west of present-day I-35 and north of the old San Antonio city limits.

On January 9, 1840, three Comanche chiefs and a Mexican captive they used for an interpreter came to the military headquarters at San Antonio and contacted Colonel Henry Wax Karnes, the commander. The gist of their story was that they weren't any better friends to the Cherokees—or the Mexicans—than the Texians were, and that though both the Cherokees and the Mexicans had attempted to enlist them in a war against the Republic, they'd refused to join in.

After telling Karnes what good boys they'd been, they then got down to business. They'd had a general council of their chiefs about two weeks earlier and decided to discuss peace terms with the Texians—probably prompted by the very effective military campaign the Texians waged against the Cherokees.

Karnes was no fool. He told the Comanches that in order to discuss peace with the Texians the Comanches would have to bring in all Texian captives they held, return all stolen property, and agree to deliver any future raiders to the Texians for punishment. Surprisingly, the Comanches agreed to the conditions, promising to return in "twenty or thirty days" to finalize the negotiations. Karnes presented them with gifts of tobacco and cloth, and they left San Antonio. The next day Karnes sent a dispatch to the Republic's Secretary of War, Dr. Branch T. Archer, telling him what was going on.

Archer didn't trust the Comanches a bit further than Karnes did. He ordered Colonel William L. Fisher, commanding the Republic's First Regiment of Infantry, to move three companies to San Antonio and be ready. If the Comanches kept their word and brought in the white captives, the soldiers were to do nothing. If they did not, the troops were to be used to hold the chiefs hostage until all the captives were brought in. Two men, Hugh McLeod (the adjutant general) and Colonel William G. Cooke, were appointed to meet with the Indians, and Karnes and the "peace commission" were instructed that no gifts would be given the Comanches at the next meeting.

It was almost two months—March 19—before Comanche scouts came back to San Antonio to inform the Texians that the Comanches were ready to talk. Shortly after there came in a party of sixty-five Comanches—the twelve big chiefs along with warriors, women, and children. They brought with them one white captive, a fifteen-year-old girl named Matilda Lockhart. The twelve chiefs were immediately taken to the old Council House, which stood at the corner of Main Plaza and what is now Market but was then Calabozo (Jail) Street. The other Indians stayed outside, and—from contemporary reports—were getting along fairly well with the locals.

Matilda Lockhart was not a good captive for the Comanches to bring in. She'd been tortured—they'd burned most of the girl's nose off, waking her up or punishing her by holding a red hot coal to her nose—and she didn't owe her captors a thing. She told the peace commission that there were a number of other captives in the Comanches' camp, and they intended to see how big a ransom they could get for her, then bring the other captives in one by one. The commission saw treachery, and treachery it was—the same kind of tricks the Comanches had been using on the Spanish and Mexicans for over a hundred years. The Texians hadn't come to play games. The troops were ordered to move up to the Council House. Then they asked the chiefs where the other captives were.

A chief named Muke-war-rah told the commission they had brought in the only one they had, the others were captured by other tribes. The commission knew this was a lie, and after a pause, Muke-war-rah asked the commissioners, "How do you like the answer?"

Colonel Fisher took over. He told Muke-war-rah—and the other chiefs—that they had lied, that the Texians knew full well they had other captives. The Texians had agreed to talk peace on the understanding that the Comanches would show good faith and bring in all the white captives, but since they hadn't . . . and then he dropped the bomb.

The women and children and the other warriors might go, he said, but the twelve chiefs were now hostages to the good treatment and return of the white captives and would not be permitted to leave until all the whites the Texians knew were in the Comanche camp were returned. The door immediately opened and an entire company of Infantry (about 60 men) marched in. Another company blockaded the back of the Council House and guards were put on the doors.

And that, as the saying goes, is when it hit the fan! The chiefs drew their knives and strung their bows and were ordered to put them down or be shot. One chief ran for the door, where he stabbed the sentry and was immediately shot down. The others rushed the soldiers and ran head-on into a volley, which left them all dead. The "fight" inside the Council House lasted about thirty seconds.

There were still fifty-three Indians outside, and when yelling and shots came from the Council House they made a break for it. The two companies of Infantry stationed outside opened fire on them, killing a good many—and, just incidentally, hitting several citizens of San Antonio who were either unfortunate or uninformed enough to be in the line of fire. Others took refuge in various stone houses around the Council House, where the soldiers rooted them out, in one case dropping a "candlewick ball soaked in turpentine and blazing" through a hole in the roof. It landed directly on a Comanche's head, and he and his companions charged out—right into the muzzles of the Infantry's muskets. Another group, heading for the river, came head-to-head with a large black woman who was in charge of a group of children, both black and white. She grabbed a huge rock, raised it above her head, and told the lead Comanche she was going to "mash his head in" with it if he didn't leave her and the children alone. Whether or not he understood the words, he certainly understood that rock—she and the children were not harmed.

When the smoke cleared, sixty-four of the sixty-five Comanches were dead or captured. The twelve chiefs, eighteen warriors, three women, and two children had been killed, while the rest—twenty-seven women and children and two old men—were locked in the jailhouse. Over 100 horses and a lot of buffalo robes and other skins were captured as well. The Texians lost seven killed—one officer and two private soldiers, three Anglo citizens, and an unknown Hispanic male who apparently wandered into the line of fire. He was never identified. Three Texian officers—one of them was Captain Mathew "Old Paint" Caldwell—and one private soldier were wounded, along with four civilians.

There followed, amazingly enough, a twelve-day truce. One of the Indian women was released, given a horse and food, and sent to the Comanche camp to tell the Indians what had happened—no doubt told to take the word that the Texians were through playing games—and to arrange for an exchange of prisoners.

On April 3 a Comanche chief named Piava and one woman came into San Antonio and told the Texians that the Comanches were ready to swap prisoners. He was given "bread, brown sugar candy cones (piloncillos), and a beef." The talking started again on April 4, and though it was touchy, the Texians finally recovered seven captives, among whom were a little girl named Putnam and a boy, Booker L. Webster. The Webster boy told the Texians that the Comanches, on hearing of the deaths of the chiefs, tortured thirteen American (Texian) captives to death. All of the captives who were returned had been tortured and maltreated, and the little Putnam girl's nose had also been badly burned.

The killing of the twelve chiefs was a major blow, and it took the Comanches a while to recover. They hung around the northern edge of San Antonio into the early summer, mostly stealing livestock and occasionally murdering a lone traveler, but the major attack the Texians were expecting didn't seem to materialize. Finally the Indians—having been joined by those prisoners the Texians had held, who escaped in ones and twos—pulled back to the north.

THE LINNVILLE RAID

"At the time of this raid the country between the Guadalupe and San Marcos, on the west, and the Colorado on the east, above a line drawn from Gonzales to La Grange, was a wilderness, while below that line it was thinly settled. Between Gonzales and Austin, on Plum Creek, were two recent settlers, Isom J. Goode [sic] and John A. Neill. From Gonzales to within a few miles of La Grange there was not a settler. There was not one between Gonzales and Bastrop, nor one between Austin and San Antonio."

L. E. Daniell
Texas: The Country And Its Men

The above quote gives you an idea of how thinly settled lower Texas was in 1840 and will let you understand why it was fairly easy for the Comanches to do what they did—to cover so much area before being detected by the settlers. Ten years later it couldn't have been done.

There were, at this time, two parties within Mexico—the Centralists, who supported Santa Anna, and everybody else, who didn't. "Everybody else" was an agglomeration of everything from Spanish Royalists and ex-Iturbide Imperialists to anarchists, but the biggest faction was the

Constitutionalists, who claimed to support the Constitution of 1824—the same one Texas claimed to support before the Revolution. Texas supported the Constitutionalists, and the main Constitution- alist rallying point in Texas was Victoria. Victoria's port was Linnville. It was through Linnville that the Constitutionalists were getting what outside supplies they got, including guns, powder, and lead.

The situation that resulted from the Council House Fight was tailor-made for the Mexicans to exploit, and they knew it. The Comanches were after revenge, and they wanted it on a big scale. Never mind that it had been their own treachery— or simple foolishness in thinking that they could treat these new white men, the Texians, as they had treated the Spanish and Mexicans before them—that caused them to lose not just warriors but chiefs—12 chiefs—in what they didn't consider a "fair fight" at all.

For the record, to the Comanches—and to vir- tually every other Indian tribe—no fight was "fair" unless they won. Their warriors' code—which was a religion of sorts—demanded that every death of a Comanche warrior at the hands of a non– Comanche, regardless of the circumstances under which the Comanche was killed, had to be avenged with one or more deaths, at the hands of Comanches, of the "tribesmen" of those who killed the warrior. It made no difference to the Comanches that ten of their warriors were trying to steal your horse, burn your house, kidnap your children, and rape your wife; if you killed two of the Comanches who were doing this, the Comanches had to kill at least two white men and preferably many more to avenge the deaths of their tribesmen. If the Comanches killed a half- dozen horse-herders because they happened to be in the way when the warriors went on a horse raid, and the Texians killed a half-dozen of the raiders in the act, that wasn't a fair trade in the eyes of the Comanches. It was an unwarranted invasion of the Comanches' right to steal horses, and they had the right to take revenge for it. If, on the other hand, settlers managed to kill all the warriors involved in a single raid, then trying to take revenge for that was considered very bad luck and the settlements usually got off scot free.

By May of 1840 the Republic's War Department had information that General Canalizo's agents were active among the Comanches, and Dr. Archer called up militia companies to be on the lookout for a major raid. Nothing happened, and nothing happened . . . and nothing happened. The militia went home. That was exactly what the spies Canalizo had in San Antonio were waiting for. After dark on August 4, 1840, a war party of about 600 Comanche and Kiowa braves and a few of Canalizo's agents came quietly down out of the red hills north of San Antonio. The longest, most massive Indian raid in Texas history began.

About noon on August 5, somewhere near present Hallettsville, the Indians came up on the first two travelers we know about. They were Dr. Joel Ponton and a young man named Tucker Foley, who were en route from Columbus to Gonzales. They were sighted by a scouting party of twenty-seven braves, who immediately took off after them.

Foley was better mounted than Dr. Ponton, and the Indians wanted his horse. They rode by the doctor, shooting as they went, and wounded him. Ponton, being an experienced frontiersman, fell off his horse and played dead, but as soon as the Indians passed he crawled into a thicket and hid.

The Indians chased Foley for three miles, and at Ponton Creek he tried to hide in the water but was found and captured. He was taken back to where Ponton fell, and when the Indians couldn't find Ponton's body, they forced Foley to call out for him. Foley was a dead man and Ponton knew it, but he didn't have any intention of dying as well, so he refused to answer. The Indians then stripped Foley naked, held him down, cut the skin off the soles of his feet, and made him run for his life. He was finally shot and scalped. This, by the way, was a favorite Comanche torture.

Once the Indians had gone, Ponton set out afoot, wounds and all, to give the alarm. He arrived in the Lavaca settlement after nightfall and told what happened. The next morning Captain Adam Zumwalt and thirty-six men set out in pursuit, and they buried Foley on the prairie where they found him.

At about the same time Zumwalt and his men were burying Foley, the Austin-to-Gonzales mail-carrier was telling Ben McCulloch, in Gonzales, about the huge southbound Indian trail he'd seen at a crossing on Plum Creek. McCulloch and twenty-four more men then set out for Big Hill (also called McClure's Hill), where they figured to cut the Indians' trail. They camped there and on the early morning of the 7th located the trail. Shortly afterwards they met up with Zumwalt and his men, who also found the trail and were following it. About noon they met yet another party, sixty men from Victoria and "Quero" (present-day Cuero), also called Blair's Settlement at the time, under John Tumlinson. That's when the men under Zumwalt and McCulloch learned that the Comanches had already made an attack on Victoria about 4:00 P.M. on the 6th. (Victoria, remember, was the Texas headquarters for the Mexican Constitutionalists, and the Mexican agents with the Comanches were Centralists.)

The Comanches, on the 6th, caught Victoria completely by surprise. The town first thought the riders were Lipans, a temporarily-friendly Apache group, come to trade. It wasn't until the lead started flying that they realized their mistake.

The people of Victoria forted up in their houses and there weren't many casualties, but the Indians drove off over 1500 head of horses and mules and a large number of cattle, and Victoria was horseless for a while afterwards. With night they backed away to Spring Creek, then about three miles out of Victoria, where they killed Varlan Richeson and two of his slaves and captured a slave girl. The next morning—unlike their usual custom of grabbing what they could and leaving the country—the Comanches attacked again. They killed a number of people and fired several houses on the outskirts of town, but by this time the citizens had armed themselves and gotten organized. The Indians ran into well-aimed rifle fire from strongpoints when they tried to go into the main part of town. They gathered up the animals they'd stolen and the other plunder and started south.

From Victoria they went to Nine-Mile Point, where they captured Mrs. Cyrus Crosby and her infant child. Later, when the child began to cry and wouldn't be quieted, they jerked the baby out of its mother's arms, threw it to the ground, speared it, and left the body where it lay. From Nine-Mile Point they turned east and raided the Clausel Ranch, wounding the owner, burning his house, and taking more horses. That night they camped on Placedo Creek on the Benavides Ranch, where they surprised a wagoner named Stephens and killed him. A lone traveler, William

G. Ewing, on his way from Linnville to Victoria,
saw their fires at night and took them for Mexican
traders. When he reached Victoria the next morning and found that he'd nearly ridden into the
biggest Comanche raiding party in history, he
went into hysterics and had to be given opium to
calm him.

At about 8:00 A.M. the Indians were spotted on
the Victoria road about two miles west of
Linnville, but the people who saw them thought at
first that they were Mexican traders. They saw
their mistake when the Comanches went into a
huge half-moon formation and charged the town,
screaming.

Nobody, of course, was expecting an Indian
attack, and nobody had a loaded gun handy. About
a dozen people were killed in a mad scramble to
get into boats and get out into the bay, where most
of the townspeople got aboard a steamboat called
Mustang and waited out the raid.

The Comanches spent all day plundering
Linnville. At least according to some sources,
they'd been told that a large shipment of guns
intended for the Mexican Constitutionalists was in
the warehouses at Linnville, but mostly what they
found was clothes. Much of this was a shipment
of hats—mostly men's top hats—and umbrellas,
owned by a merchant named James Robinson in
San Antonio, waiting to be shipped to him as soon
as wagons could be found to ship it. Citizens waiting out the raid aboard the *Mustang* could see
Indians wearing plug or "beegum" hats, as top
hats were called, holding umbrellas over their
heads, and riding among the burning buildings of
the town. By nightfall, having killed most of the
cattle in the Linnville area, burned most of the
buildings, and destroyed everything they couldn't

kill or burn, the Comanches began to head for the red hills and home.

While all of this was going on, the Texians who'd been following the Comanches weren't idle. They knew Linnville—or somewhere—was going to be burned and sacked, and there wasn't too much they could do about that. About the only hope they had was to catch the Indians off guard, after they'd done their raiding and gotten their loot, and try to ambush them on the way home. The Comanches had the available troops outnumbered at least three to one, and going nose-to-nose with them was not a way to go home and tell folks you'd whipped the Injuns.

Tumlinson and his 125 men left Victoria and headed out on the Texana road, where they camped at the Casa Blanca waterhole and sent word to Texana for more help. They figured the Indians would come somewhere close to them on their way back north, and they weren't wrong. A little before noon on the 9th they spotted the Comanches on the west bank of Garcitas Creek.

At this point Tumlinson's flankers found themselves with the main body of Indians between them and Tumlinson's main force, and—wisely—they kept low. Tumlinson split his forces into two wings, and they began to advance—companies from Gonzales and Lavaca on the right, Victoria and Cuero on the left. The rear-guard of the Indians turned to meet the Texians.

Tumlinson's volunteers dismounted in the open prairie and the Indians moved to surround them, but the accurate rifle-fire of the Texians caused them to lose several men, while the Texians only lost one, Benjamin Mordecai of Victoria. The main body of the Indians continued to retreat, and shortly the rear guard followed, with Tumlinson's men in pursuit. The next day

Captain Clarke Owen and 40 men from Texana joined Tumlinson, and the combined command—about 160 strong, but without fresh horses, while the Indians had all the horses taken at Victoria and Linnville—began to follow the raiders.

The Tumlinson party followed for about 20 miles without another fight, and Ben McCulloch, Alsey S. Miller, Archibald Gipson, and Barney Randell left the party and headed for Gonzales. They intended to raise more men and set an ambush at Plum Creek.

All the while messengers had been going out. From up on the Lavaca, Lafayette Ward and 22 men headed for Big Hill to look for the trail but missed it. They went on to Gonzales, where they joined with a group under Mathew "Old Paint" Caldwell. Caldwell was convinced that the Comanches would cross the Guadalupe at present New Braunfels, and he, Ward, and their men went to Seguin. They were found there by another messenger, who brought the news that the Comanches were going home almost exactly by the route they'd taken to come out, and they could be caught at Plum Creek. They left Seguin and rode hard for the Gonzales-Austin road, where—at Isham Good's homestead—they met Major General Felix Huston, commander of the Texas Militia, and his aide, James Izod. The force went to Plum Creek to prepare an ambush and found Captain James Bird and 30 men from Gonzales already there. Camp was made and sentries were posted.

McCulloch, meanwhile, had split his companions up as messengers. McCulloch himself went to Gonzales, where he helped gather Bird's volunteers and then went solo-scouting to keep track of the Indians. He sent Miller looking for Old Paint, while Gipson was sent to the Colorado to find Edward Burleson. Burleson gathered 87

Texians and 13 unmounted Tonkawa braves and headed for Good's Crossing on Plum Creek, where the ambush was to be sprung.

At Good's Crossing the Texians had Caldwell and Ward's 63 men, Bird's 30 Gonzales volunteers, Ben McCulloch and his messengers, Huston and his aide, and Isham Good, for a total of 100—to go up against between 500 and 600 well-mounted Comanches. Burleson and his 100 arrived a matter of minutes before the ambush was sprung, bringing the Texians to 200.

On the morning of the 11th, before Burleson arrived, the Texians decided on an overall commander, and most of the men favored Old Paint Caldwell. He was ready—he told the men that they were but 87 strong (several were out scouting) and there were somewhere between 800 and 1000 Indians, but "I believe we can whip hell out of 'em! Boys, shall we fight?" The answer was favorable, and Caldwell immediately asked that overall command be given to General Huston, which was done, though Caldwell was the leader the men preferred to follow.

Huston moved the men out and located an ambush point. There the volunteers were overtaken by two men from Bastrop, who told Huston that Burleson was only a few minutes away and coming in as fast as possible. Huston paused long enough to allow Burleson to get in, then set up an ambush on the prairie where the Indians were expected—and where, according to the scouts who kept coming in, they would arrive any minute. The Texians formed three sides of a square, with Burleson and his men on the right side, Caldwell commanding the left, and the top of the box closed by Bird's and Ward's men under Major Thomas Hardeman. The Texians took their places and lay down in the grass to wait.

It didn't take long for the war party—warriors, women, children, some old men, and 2000 to 3000 horses stolen at various points, the line stretching for more than three miles—to walk into the trap. The Indians had dressed themselves in the clothing stolen from Linnville. Some were wearing gaudy women's dresses, and the ponies were decorated with ribbons and bolts of bright cloth. One was rigged out in full white-man finery: he had his clawhammer coat on backwards, a top hat on his head, fine boots and gloves—but of course no pants—and he was carrying an umbrella open over his head. His horse was wearing an American-made bridle, and he'd tied about ten feet of ribbon to its tail.

The Texians in the grass were checking their flints, cocking their rifles, picking their targets, and setting their triggers. The Battle of Plum Creek was about to begin.

It almost didn't happen. A small squad of volunteers, not associated with the large command under Huston, happened upon the Comanches' advance guard, almost at the last minute, and attacked them. The main war party came up; the new volunteers saw what they were up against and made a break for cover. The Comanches followed them, killed one, and chased the others off.

It was too late to spring the trap. Huston ordered his men to mount up and go after the Indians, and there was a running skirmish for about five miles. As the Texians closed on the main body, the Comanches halted to make a fight at Kelley Springs. Huston advanced his men, mounted, to within about 150 yards of the Indians, ordered them to dismount and form their hollow square, and then to advance.

Felix Huston was a brave, likeable man, but he didn't know beans about fighting Indians. The

Comanches sent out a force of 20 or 30 warriors to annoy the Texians while the others tried to make good their retreat. One of the prominent warriors of this group had an especially good shield which was stopping bullets as he charged toward the Texians. Each time he stopped, the shield would fly up, exposing his body momentarily. The Texians waited for his next charge and, when the shield flew up, riddled him with bullets. They then got several more warriors who were trying to rescue his body. He was apparently a fairly important war chief, for McCulloch and Caldwell recognized the grief cries of the Indians from the woods where the man was taken. Both of the seasoned Indian fighters began to press Huston to order the men to mount and charge.

About 90 percent of all 19th century military thought was based on either defense or caution. It was not a bad idea when fighting a set-piece battle against neat rows of Infantry advancing across a European battlefield, but against Indians it just didn't work. Felix Huston had never, before coming to Texas, commanded men or been in a war. All he knew he got from listening to people who had been trained to fight in the classic European tradition. Again, he didn't know beans about fighting Indians. Fortunately, however, he seems to have been the sort of feller who didn't mind listening to those who did know what they were talking about, and in Ben McCulloch and Old Paint Caldwell he had two of the best in the business. If McCulloch and Caldwell said "Charge," then—against his own judgement—Felix Huston would order a charge. He did.

The charge by the Texians ended all semblance of organized resistance on the part of the Comanches. From then on, their purpose seemed to be only to get away as fast as possible with as much loot and as many horses as they could. One group, driving a great number of pack animals, ran into a boggy creek bottom, where most of the pack animals became mired. According to one participant, the animals were so jammed together "you could have walked across the creek dry." Many of the pack horses were loaded with iron barrel hoops—from which the Comanches intended to make iron arrowheads.

Alsey Miller was armed with a peculiar seven-shot repeating musket. It had a cylinder like a Colt, but instead of being rotated automatically, it had to be rotated by hand. Miller failed, in the heat of battle, to rotate the cylinder far enough, and his gun misfired. The Indian he was after, who was charging toward him, had an arrow to his bowstring when Miller reversed his musket and whacked the warrior one upside the head with the butt, causing him to drop both bow and arrow. The Comanche jerked a handful of arrows from his quiver and attempted to stab Miller with them, but Miller ducked the stabs until he had the gun's cylinder correctly aligned, then blew the warrior's head off.

Ben McCulloch and Dr. Alonzo B. Sweitzer, also present at the battle, cordially hated each others' guts. McCulloch was reloading his rifle when an Indian rode up on him. Before the Indian could strike, Sweitzer killed him. McCulloch said nothing, but within five minutes he killed a Comanche who'd caught Sweitzer in a similar bind. Neither man spoke to the other while this was happening.

Andrew Jackson Sowell shot a Comanche's horse out from under him. The Comanche landed on his feet, ran a few steps, then turned back to try and take the bridle—a fairly common one, worth about $2—off the dead horse. Sowell shot at him and the bullet struck the Comanche's shield, but before he could get away another Texian nailed him.

One old, apparently fairly prominent chief was hit several times in the head, his head being "nearly blown off." Apparently he'd tied himself in his saddle or he'd gotten a "death grip" with his hands and knees, because though he was shot and hit with butts of Texian muskets several times, he remained in the saddle. His horse carried him into some woods and the mystery of how he stayed mounted with most of his head gone was never solved.

The Comanches, of course, tried to kill all their captives—a regular practice when they were having to retreat in a hurry. Mrs. Cyrus Crosby— she was a granddaughter of Daniel Boone—whose baby they'd murdered near Victoria, was shot with two arrows which went completely through her body, and she survived only hours. She was buried on the battlefield after the fighting ended. In 1850 the Lockhart Masonic Lodge removed her remains and reburied her, but no one seems to know exactly where.

Mrs. Hugh O. Watts, who had been taken at Linnville—her husband was killed there—was found with an arrow in her breast. Rev. Morrell and Dr. David F. Brown of Bastrop finally extracted it with the Reverend holding the woman's hands at her sides—she'd refused to let go of the arrow shaft—while Dr. Brown grabbed the shaft and simply pulled it loose. The arrow's iron head was bent—it had struck the steel boning in her corset and been deflected—which made it painful to remove but kept it from killing her.

Among the plunder recovered on the battlefield was not merely horses, mules, and drygoods, but large quantities of books and a number of small baby alligators. It was a long time before white men discovered what use the Comanches had for books, but books were taken in almost every raid in which they were found. The Comanches lined the insides of their war shields with thick books—an outer layer of buffalo rawhide, a stick framework, an inner layer of thick books, another stick framework, and a rear layer of buffalo rawhide would stop all but a close-range shot from the most powerful of frontier rifles. The why behind the baby alligators was never discovered, though many Texians speculated that the Comanches had taken them to prove they really had been as far as the Gulf Coast on a raid. They also carried what the Texians described as "large portions of human flesh, apparently prepared for cooking," though no other report ever implies that the Comanches might have engaged in cannibalism.

Mrs. Watts reported that the Comanches had whipped and abused Mrs. Crosby fiercely, calling her a "peon," because she could not read the books to them. Mrs. Watts had been forced to read passages from the books to the Indians and explain the pictures inside.

The Tonkawas, who were identified by strips of white cloth tied around their upper arms, may have come to the fight afoot but they didn't stay that way long. Within a few minutes every Tonkawa was mounted on a Comanche pony, and amid the shooting of the Texians, the Tonks were tomahawking and stabbing Comanches as fast as they could catch up to them. After the battle, Robert Hall, who'd been wounded, was resting on a pallet when the Tonks built a large fire near him. They then dragged up the body of a Comanche warrior, which they proceeded to butcher, roast, and eat. Hall reported that he was offered a slice of broiled Comanche but, though he was very hungry, he wasn't that hungry.

Most of the loot—but by no means all—was recovered after the battle, but much of it couldn't be identified and was split among the men as "spoils of war." Some of it the Comanches apparently attempted to bury. A group of slave girls saw a small band of warriors burying something, but were unable later, because they were so frightened, to point out where they'd seen the Indians bury whatever it was.

The Comanches lost between 60 and 70 warriors and chiefs on the battlefield at Plum Creek, and another 20 to 30 died of wounds and were buried or abandoned later. Over the years Comanche bones, apparently dating from the Plum Creek fight, were found as far north as the San Antonio Road. The Texians lost one man killed —a Mr. DeWolf—and seven wounded: Robert Hall, Henry McCulloch, Archibald Gipson, Columbus DeWitt, Dr. Alonzo B. Sweitzer, James Nichols, and Samuel H. Reed.

After Plum Creek the Comanches never again made a major raid into the settled parts of Texas. They also never again trusted a Mexican governmental agent. Of all the things they'd gotten on the raid, the one thing they were after above all else— guns—was the one thing they didn't find.

Copied from a very early, badly faded print on glass, this never-before-published photo shows Joseph Woods (1802-1880?), veteran of San Jacinto and Plum Creek. He later led the unauthorized foray deep into enemy-held territory during the Mexican War to exhume, collect, and return to Texas the bones of the Mier Expedition martyrs. The rifle or shotgun Woods is holding is unidentifiable, but may be a very rare multibarreled rifle.

This never-before-published photo, computer-enhanced from an extremely dim original, shows Ashel (also spelled Azael and Aziel) Dancer (on the right, with beard), a Tennesseean born in 1795, who fought in the battles of Horsehoe Bend and New Orleans in the War of 1812 and later fought at Plum Creek. This may be the oldest surviving photograph ever taken in Texas. "Colonel" Dancer was killed by Indians in 1849. There is no historically recorded photography in Texas before the early 1850s.

Both photos from the family collection of Victor Woods, Seguin, Texas.

THE LEGEND OF THE
YELLOW ROSE

Now let's back up just a mite. We all know that
Sam Houston and the Texican army won at San
Jacinto—but how? What caused an army run by a
pretty good field commander—which Santa Anna
was—to be caught with its britches down in the
middle of hostile country?

To most people—and that includes nearly all
Texans—"The Yellow Rose of Texas" is nothing
more than a song once sung by cowboys on the
long trails from Texas to Kansas in the 1880s. It is
considered a lament for the lost affections of
some—probably imaginary—rancher's or farmer's
daughter the cowboy intends to return to "when
the work's all done this fall" and if he ever gets
around to it and she ain't married yet.

When, in the 1940s, Roy Rogers took the old
folksong/cowboy ballad to build a movie title
around, he removed it entirely from even the cowboy tradition. Roy's "Yellow Rose of Texas" was a
paddle-wheeler riverboat which, judging from its
size, had to be somewhere on the Mississippi,
since no Texas river has been navigable by boats of
that size since well before 1900. With typical
Republic Pictures disregard for history, realism,

continuity, how many times a sixshooter will shoot without reloading, or what happens to a feller's white hat when somebody lands a hay-maker on his chin, *The Yellow Rose of Texas* embraced raging sixshooter battles, horseback chases, and wagonloads of gold bullion, as well as automobiles, telephones, gangsters, and ballistic matching of bullets.

There was a line in the song that gave Roy some trouble, so he changed it. When Dale Evans—play-ing, as usual, the beautiful spitfire daughter of the unjustly accused old codger (Gabby Hayes, of course) whom Roy proves innocent—sat on the upper rail of the Yellow Rose's promenade deck to listen, Roy sang "She's the sweetest little rosebud this cowboy ever knew." He sang that because the original line from the ca. 1840 Tin Pan Alley minstrel song went "She's the sweetest rose of color this darky ever knew." The song, when it first became popular, was a fixture in blackface minstrel shows, and it was understood that the "Yellow Rose" was so named from her color—she was a quadroon or octoroon girl.

There really was a Yellow Rose of Texas, and she was truly "yellow," for persons of the par-ticular mixture of white and black races that she carried in her genes have a distinct yellowish cast to their skins. Her name was Emily, and she was an indentured servant on the plantation of James Morgan, an early settler at the village of New Washington, on a peninsula known as Morgan's Point, which juts into San Jacinto Bay a few miles south of present-day Houston.

Morgan's Emily, by which name she was known in 1836, came from Mississippi with her owner, James Morgan, at the invitation of the Mexican government in the early 1830s. The Mexican government had abolished Negro slavery

—but only in the Province of Texas, please note. It was quite legal to own slaves, be they black, Indian, or mestizo, anywhere else in Mexico, and the practice of peonage, which was *de facto* slavery, was not banned anywhere in Mexico. James Morgan, like many Southern immigrants to Texas, had much of his fortune tied up in slaves. Morgan freed all his slaves with a single stroke of a pen and indentured them as servants for a period of 99 years with another stroke. This neat fiction Mexico accepted completely. To the slaves, one type of slavery was about the same as another.

Emily has been described variously as mulatto (half black, half white), quadroon (one-fourth black), and octoroon (one-eighth black). When, in my childhood, the "little old ladies" of Texas history could be persuaded to talk about her at all—and that wasn't often—they referred to her in much less complimentary terms. Mexican chroniclers call her "Santa Anna's quadroon mistress." Contemporary descriptions indicate that she had finely chiseled, extremely attractive features; coal black, wavy hair; dark brown eyes; and a "golden" cast to her skin. The description is that of an octoroon.

While her ancestry is questionable, her beauty and sex appeal are not. There are any number of stories about the effect Emily had on the young men of New Washington. It is safe to say that Emily was capable of catching a man's eye—and quite a bit more—anytime she wanted to, and she apparently wanted to quite often. One of the stories—both historically and ballistically impossible, by the way—insists that the merchants of New Washington petitioned James Morgan to forbid Emily to walk down the streets of the town. It seemed that every time she did, it cost them money—their expensive glass show-windows were being shattered by the fly buttons of those young men who watched her progress from across the street. While this is impossible—there weren't any glass show-windows in New Washington (or anywhere else in Texas) until the 1850s, and the ballistic coefficient of even a metal flybutton is such that it wouldn't shatter glass at any noticeable range—the story well illustrates Emily's effect on the libidos of most of those males who saw her. It is claimed that by the time Emily was 21 she had enjoyed every male over the age of 16 who lived within 20 miles of New Washington, and there seems to be little reason to doubt the tradition.

Any story that begins with a beautiful and sensuous woman must have a man to fall under her spell. The man in this story was a pure-blooded Spanish Criollo (a "creole"—one of pure European ancestry but born in the New World) named Antonio Lopez, whose father's family came from a region called Santa Ana in Spain, and whose mother's family—the "y Perez" part of his name—came from the village of LeBron, near the Spanish-French border. To give him his full name and honorifics, at the time he became entangled in the thorns of the Yellow Rose he was Excelencio, Presidente de la República de Méjico, Generalísimo y Comandante de los Ejercitos de la República de Méjico, Don Antonio López de Santa Ana y Pérez de LeBrón—better known to Texas as General Santa Anna, the self-styled "Napoleon of the West."

Santa Anna, by best information, was born in Jalapa, Mexico, in 1794. His father intended him for a career as a merchant. He showed a remarkable ineptitude for commerce but great interest in a military career. In 1810, at the age of 16, he entered the Royal Spanish Army as a cadet officer. He proved to be a natural soldier, not merely adept at both tactics and strategy—he was a gifted and

astute student of military history and strategy—
but personally brave almost to the point of
recklessness. In ten years—an astoundingly short
time in the Spanish Colonial Army—he had risen
to the rank of lieutenant colonel. What's more he
did it on merit, not on family money, making his
rise all the more astounding.

In 1820, in the last stages of the Mexican
Revolution of 1810-1821, he personally planned
and executed a remarkably effective battle which
virtually exterminated almost an entire province's
revolutionary army. On the strength of his
expertise and record, he confidently expected to
be promoted to colonel, with a general's rank in
the not-distant future. Instead his gauchupin
(espanole gauchupin, not criollo gauchupin)
superiors told him that he had risen as far as any
mere criollo had any right to expect to rise in the
army. The coveted colonelcy went to a gauchupin
who was not merely far inferior to Santa Anna
militarily, but a personal enemy of the young
criollo lieutenant colonel as well. Santa Anna
bided his time, and at a critical moment in the
next battle, he suddenly switched sides with his
entire command, bringing a very important
victory to the Mexican Republicans and making
himself a hero of the Republic's cause.

Out of the chaos that resulted in Mexican
politics following the ouster of Spain, Santa Anna
emerged as one of the most potent forces in the
new republic. From the fall of former Republican
general Augustín Iturbide, the self-crowned
Iturbide I, Emperor of Mexico—in whose fall Santa
Anna had a very large hand—until the aftermath of
the U.S.-Mexican war of 1846-47, Antonio López
de Santa Ana y Pérez de LeBrón was the single
most powerful man in Mexico, either holding the

presidency himself or naming (and often remov-
ing by force) the man who did.

Santa Anna's self-given nickname, "The
Napoleon of the West," was no idle thing. He
envisioned Mexico as the Napoleonic France of the
Americas. His long-range vision saw Mexico con-
trolling the entire Gulf of Mexico and Caribbean
through conquest of Cuba, the remaining
Caribbean islands, all of Central America, the entire north coast of South America, and—most
likely—the former Spanish colonies of Louisiana,
Mississippi, Alabama, and Florida.

Santa Anna was not universally loved and
respected in Mexico, though. At least one Mexican
statesman, on hearing of Santa Anna's proposal to
invade and conquer Cuba, suggested that Mexico
certainly could not lose in the process. Either
Santa Anna would take Cuba, he explained, or the
Spanish would defeat, capture, and execute him.
Either result would be of immeasurable benefit to
Mexico.

Like many Central and South American political figures—and to judge by some recent
presidential campaigns, not a few North American
ones—Santa Anna considered himself God's gift to
women and went to great pains to prove that he
had an apparently insatiable appetite for beautiful
women. Whether or not all his boasting was true,
he did manage to accumulate, during his life, a
string of mistresses long enough to qualify him for
the *Guinness Book of World Records* if Guinness
recognized the category of "World's Champion
Womanizer." What his beautiful and long-suffer-
ing wife, Doña Ines, thought of his extra-marital
adventures history doesn't record.

When Santa Anna marched out of Mexico in
February of 1836 to teach the upstart Texicans a
lesson, he left not merely Doña Ines but his entire

retinue of women behind. When he arrived in San Antonio to besiege the fortress the Texicans under William Barret Travis and James Bowie had made of the old Mission San Antonio de Valero—sometimes called "El Alamo" for the cottonwood trees that grew along the banks of its irrigation ditch— he had been without a woman for almost a month. While his staff—most particularly his chief of staff, Colonel Juan Valentin Amador—prepared and directed the siege, The Napoleon of the West went woman-hunting.

He found a beautiful and virtuous 17-year-old girl named Melchora Iniega Barrera living with her widowed mother in a capacious house that he felt would make an ideal headquarters. Santa Anna moved in, bag, baggage, and staff, and began to pay court to the innocent Melchora.

The girl resisted the dictator's gifts, attentions, blandishments, and—ultimately—threats, insisting that the only way to her bed was through marriage. Finally, instead of forcing her and having done with it, Santa Anna found, among his troops, an Irishman who had once been an actor. The Irishman dressed in priestly robes, dispensed with the usual formalities of banns, and performed a sham marriage. While the Battle of the Alamo raged in earshot of the Barrera home, Santa Anna enjoyed his 17-year-old "bride."

The Alamo fell on March 6. By the 15th the Mexican army had regrouped, been resupplied with ammunition from Mexico, and was fully ready to go play chase with the ragtag-and-bobtail Texicans under Sam Houston. Santa Anna, however, was too entranced with his new toy, Melchora, to be bothered with such things as military campaigns. This gave Sam Houston a much-needed opportunity to move closer to his supply lines, which were coming out of Louisiana.

On the morning of March 31 the Mexican army marched out of San Antonio, flags flying and bands playing, and Santa Anna was on his way to crush the "upstart Norteamericanos"—with, of course, his latest toy along to keep him amused. By April 3 it was raining floods, the going was rough, and Santa Anna sent most of his personal loot—including Melchora—back with a trusted aide, resigning himself to a celibate life in his pure-silk campaign tent.

By April 18 celibacy had lost any appeal it ever had, and at just about that time the Mexican army marched into the village of New Washington at Morgan's Point—which just happened to be the home of James Morgan and, of course, Morgan's Emily, soon to be The Yellow Rose of Texas. At this point formal history fails us and legend and tradition take over.

Tradition holds that Sam Houston, knowing of Santa Anna's appetite for beautiful women, approached James Morgan about the already-somewhat-legendary Emily. If the girl could be slipped into Santa Anna's camp, Houston reckoned, it wouldn't be long before such a beautiful and obviously sensual woman came to the dictator's notice. If Emily could keep Santa Anna as occupied out in the open as Melchora had in San Antonio—a small task for a woman of Emily's undoubted talents—Santa Anna just might be caught off guard when he most needed to be on guard, and the Texas army might have a better-than-even chance of taking his forces by surprise while the general was "otherwise occupied." Speed, though, was essential. If the highly competent Martín Perfectó de Cós, Santa Anna's brother-in-law, arrived with his 1250 fresh troops before the Texicans could attack, the odds would tip greatly in favor of the Mexicans.

Emily was approached with what was presented to her as a no-lose proposition. If she would
seduce the handsome 41-year-old "Napoleon of the
West" and the Texicans defeated him, Emily
would be honored as the woman who helped to
save Texas, given a substantial share of any treasure captured from the Mexican army, and—most
important, at least from Emily's point of view—
given her freedom. If the Texicans lost, there
was no reason anyone, least of all Santa Anna,
should ever know just why she came into his life
when she did, and Santa Anna was known to be
extremely generous to his mistresses. Either way,
Emily came out of the fight rich and free.

She wasted no time at all. By the evening of the
18th she was sharing Santa Anna's silk tent. His
personal aide, Colonel Pedro Delgado, records that
on the morning of the 19th, while the army began
its march, Santa Anna remained abed with his
"quadroon mistress."

Apparently Emily managed to put the fear of
God—or at least of Sam Houston—into him in the
process, for at about 10 A.M. the army was very
nearly stampeded when the terrified Santa Anna,
suddenly realizing that he was between his own
army and the Texicans, came tearing through the
ranks on a white horse, screaming "The enemy are
coming! The enemy are coming!" at the top of his
lungs. It took, according to Mexican army reports,
almost three hours to undo the confusion and get
the army underway again.

Santa Anna enjoyed himself with Emily on the
night of the 19th and again on the night of the
20th, and on the morning of the 21st he put
his army into encampment on a slight rise in
the saltgrass prairie along the sluggish Rio San
Jacinto. At about 10 A.M. the worst possible thing,
from the Texican point of view, that could have

happened on that or any other day, happened. De Cós arrived with his troops. Fortunately, Santa Anna was so preoccupied that he could do no more than leave his tent for a few minutes, tell de Cós to allow his troops a good rest, and then return.

Exactly what was happening inside the silken bower history does not record, but we do know that while the Mexican army camped, for all intents and purposes leaderless, on the plain of St. Hyacinth, Santa Anna remained in his tent. Why?

In his own rationalization for his defeat, published some months later, Santa Anna stated that he was having a nap—a siesta. According to Texas historian R. Henderson Shuffler, it might better have been termed a "fiesta."

At about 3:30 P.M. all hell broke loose. Two small cannon suddenly began to rain broken horseshoes, chopped-up chain, nails, bolts, and broken glass among the Mexican lines, and the dozing camp was abruptly filled with buckskin-clad Texicans swinging long knives and clubbed rifles and screaming "Remember the Alamo! Remember Goliad!" Colonel Delgado recorded in his memoirs that he saw Santa Anna immediately after the attack began. The president of Mexico ran out of his silk tent clad only in a linen shirt and silk drawers, saw the oncoming Texicans, and began to wring his hands and dance around como un loco (like a nut). Without issuing a single order, he seized a horse the army had captured a few days before, leaped into the saddle, and rode away at a mad gallop.

The Battle of San Jacinto, today considered the sixteenth decisive battle in world history, ended in eighteen minutes. As a result of it and its aftermath, Mexico lost not merely Texas, but New Mexico, Arizona, California, Nevada, Utah, and parts of Oklahoma, Wyoming, Colorado, and Kansas—something in excess of a million square miles of territory. The political face of North America was utterly changed, and with it, the history of the world. The Napoleon of the West, and with him his dream of a Caribbean Empire, was finished. Which, as Henderson Shuffler has commented, was probably the world's record price for what, in part, Santa Anna got in exchange.

What of Emily, The Yellow Rose of Texas, who traded her talents and abilities for one-fourth of the present continental United States? Nobody knows. Emily never again appears in history or legend. There is a record that one of the "Mexican camp-followers" was found dead on the field, apparently killed in the confusion, but there is no description of the body. Romantic legend—and it's no more than that—insists that Santa Anna realized, at the last instant, what the woman had done and knifed her in his tent. No official history mentions Emily, and even the Morgan family has no records or traditions to indicate what happened to her. The only semiofficial mention she gets is in the memoirs of George Erath, for whom Erath County is named, when he says that the Mexican army was defeated as much by Santa Anna's "voluptuousness" as anything else.

There's no monument to Emily at San Jacinto, and perhaps there should be one. Several Texas historians—the late Henderson Shuffler being one—suggested that an appropriate one would be a reclining nude female statue carved of golden-hued stone.

Needless to say, such a monument hasn't been—and isn't likely to be—erected at San Jacinto. Emily, though, has a monument that will, in all likelihood, outlast any granite or bronze. It begins:

WILBARGER

This, in a sense, is my personal ghost story —though I share it with a lot of kin, both blood and kissin'. My grandmother, Mary Ann Lane Eckhardt, was born at Hornsby Bend, Texas in 1873, and this is one of the tales she grew up on. She passed it on to me back in the days before television, and I passed it on to my daughter.

Josiah Wilbarger came to Texas from Indiana sometime in the 1820s, then settled at a place called Hornsby Bend, on the Colorado River, just below the struggling community of Waterloo. Both Waterloo and Hornsby Bend are parts of Austin now, but if you'll go look at a map of Austin, you notice that the Colorado makes a large bend just below the Montopolis Bridge in the southeast part of Texas' capital city. That's Hornsby Bend, and it was there that pioneer settler Reuben Hornsby brought his wife Sarah and their children and erected a blockhouse fort in the 1820s.

Wilbarger was a single man, a scout and frontiersman with a reputation as a guide. Seeing as he was sweet on one of the Hornsby daughters, he spent a lot of time in the vicinity of Hornsby's Fort when he wasn't out scouting or guiding parties of surveyors or landhunters. The fort became his unofficial headquarters, and it was from Hornsby's

Fort that he preferred to leave for the wild country. He left there early one April morning in 1832, guiding a party of surveyors up the Colorado into the unclaimed country beyond settlement. There were, depending on who tells the tale, anywhere from eight to a dozen in the party.

The road was predictable—up the banks of Onion Creek—and that was the problem. Wilbarger made the mistake no guide in hostile country, no frontiersman, no soldier, and no police officer should ever make. He fell into a rut, doing things by habit. When you do things by habit others can observe your habits and use them to your disadvantage.

It was still early morning and the party was no more than six or eight miles from the fort when Wilbarger's carelessness caught up with him and his surveyors. Indians—probably Comanches— waylaid the trail he had come to use by force of habit. A volley of gunfire and arrows from the brush emptied all but the two tail-end saddles, and the last two men turned tail and ran for the fort. The Indians ignored them and fell on the rest.

Wilbarger was hit in the neck by a very-large-caliber but apparently slow-moving musket ball. It bruised, but did not break, both the carotid artery and the jugular vein and passed between the man's throat and his spine, apparently bruising without breaking his spinal column. He fell from his horse, dead—or so he appeared. In fact, he was fully conscious but unable to move or speak, the impact of the bullet having paralyzed him temporarily but completely. This is called "creasing" and is usually done by shooting across the spinal column but not through it. A lot of mustangs were captured by "creasing" and temporarily paralyzing them. A lot more mustangs were killed because the feller trying to do the creasing wasn't anywhere near as good a shot as he thought he was. The accidental "creasing" was what saved Wilbarger's life.

The Indians immediately began to strip and scalp the men. When Wilbarger's turn came, he later recalled, he felt pressure on his scalp but no pain as the Indian cut around the hair and skin he intended to remove. Wilbarger heard a sound "like distant thunder" as the scalp was ripped from his head. He was unable to react in any way, though he later said that he was looking the Indian directly in the eyes at the time he was lifted up by his hair and was conscious during the whole procedure. Had he moved or blinked, he later said, he would have been killed immediately, but the impact of the bullet in his neck had deadened all his senses and made it impossible for him even to blink his eyes.

At some point in the proceedings Wilbarger lost consciousness, and when he awoke he could once more move and speak. He was lying naked, save for one sock, on the banks of Onion Creek. Horses, guns, clothing, and anything else the white men had with them was gone. He crawled to the edge of the creek, washed the blood off his face, got a drink of water, and then took off his sock, soaked it in the cold water of the creek, and laid it over the bare bone where his scalp had been torn away. Finally, he struggled to his feet and began to move, half crawling, half stumbling, in the direction of Hornsby's Fort.

He covered perhaps a mile from the site of the ambush, sometimes crawling, sometimes in a stumbling walk. Darkness overtook him near a huge liveoak tree on the bank of the creek. Knowing that he had gone as far as he could and expecting to die at any moment, he sat down under the tree, "composed myself as decently as I could" (probably meaning he crossed his hands on his crotch), and waited to die.

As he lay there, the form of his sister, back home in Indiana, appeared before him. "Have no fear, Brother Josiah," she said. "Help is on the way." She then "disappeared from my sight, going in the direction of Hornsby's Fort." The time was probably about 6 P.M. or a little after, just before twilight becomes dark, and Wilbarger was about six miles or a little more from the Hornsby home.

In 1832 in rural Texas folks got up with the chickens—and went to bed with them as well. Lamp oil and candles were too expensive and too hard to come by to waste by sitting up late at night. The Hornsbys were probably in bed by 7 P.M. or a little later. At a little after 8 P.M.—she later said she'd been asleep about an hour—Sarah Hornsby suddenly sat bolt upright in bed. She'd had a dream—a very vivid dream. She saw Wilbarger, naked and wounded but alive—contrary to the statement of the two escapees from the massacre, who insisted that all were killed—lying under a big tree on the bank of a creek.

Reuben Hornsby was a no-nonsense sort of a feller. He told the woman she was just dreaming, to go back to sleep. She did. The dream came a second time, this time with greater detail. Wilbarger had been scalped, she told her husband, but had laid a cloth of some sort over the place where his hair had been torn loose. She got the same reaction from Reuben and went back to sleep again.

The third time the dream came she was not going to go back to sleep. Wilbarger, she said, was alive. He'd put a sock over the place where his scalp had been torn off. She described the tree— well known to her husband—and told him he'd find Wilbarger under it, sitting with his back to the tree, naked and bloody but still alive. He wouldn't be able to ride, she said, so the men must take the wagon and pad it with plenty of quilts and blankets.

Though Reuben Hornsby no doubt thought his wife was out of her ever-lovin' mind, it was pretty obvious to him that if he and his boys planned to get any sleep that April night, they were going to have to humor her. Reuben roused the older boys, hitched up the wagon, provided themselves with lanterns and guns, and set out up the banks of Onion Creek. Just about six miles from the house they found Josiah Wilbarger just as Sarah had described him.

Josiah Wilbarger later married one of the Hornsby daughters and retired from being a frontiersman. He operated a cotton gin near Hornsby Bend for the rest of his life. The skin never grew back where he'd been scalped, and he wore a quilted skullcap over the spot. In 1845, while coming out of his gin, he struck his forehead on the lintel of a low door and fractured his skull. He died within days. Wilbarger County, Texas, is named for him.

Remember that sister who appeared to Josiah? As far as Josiah knew, she was perfectly healthy at the time. Some seven or eight months later he received a letter from his family in Indiana. His sister had been taken ill with "the fevers"—one of the many fever-symptomed diseases that abounded in the days before antibiotics and immunizations—and died. She died the day before he was ambushed. As he lay unconscious on the banks of Onion Creek, her family laid her to rest in Indiana. As she appeared to him, she was spending her first night in the grave. It takes, by actual test, about two and a half hours to walk from the tree where Wilbarger was found to the site of

Hornsby's Fort—which is just about, so far as we can tell from the narrative, the same time that elapsed between the appearance of his sister to Josiah Wilbarger and Sarah Hornsby's first dream. Coincidence? You decide.

THE GHOST AT BAILEY'S PRAIRIE

If you've got to have a ghost around the place, it's best to have a jolly one. Even better is to have one that doesn't mind a nip at a jug of sour mash.

James Britton Bailey came to Texas from South Carolina, in the early days of Anglo immigration, and settled on a tract of land between present-day East Columbia and West Columbia, between the San Bernard and the Brazos rivers in present-day Brazoria County. He named the tract "Bailey's Prairie," and there he built a large sawlumber house which he painted a dark, barn-paint red. He was a typical Texas frontiersman, hardbitten and plain-spoken, but there was nothing really notable about him—until he died.

Brit Bailey, as he was known to his neighbors, married and raised a typical brood of children, and then in 1832 he succumbed to "the fevers"— the exact nature of "the fevers" is unspecified—and died. He was apparently pretty lucid during his last day or so on earth, for he gave specific directions for his burial. He insisted that he was to be buried standing up, "for I never lied to a man in my life, and I want no man, on passing my grave, to say 'there lies old Brit Bailey.'" He wanted to be buried with his face to the west, for he had begun going west when he left Carolina and had never ceased to look to the setting sun. He wanted to be buried with his rifle at his side; with a full horn of powder and his pouch filled with bullets and fresh flints; with his possibles bag filled with pipe, tobacco, strike-a-light, and chaw; and with a full jug of whiskey at his feet. "For," he said, "a man doesn't know how long the road may be and what hazards may be along it, and my rifle has never failed me yet, and I may be in need of refreshment along the way." He died—and this is recorded fact— on October 31, 1832.

Brit Bailey's funeral was preached, appropriately enough, by a local priest of the Roman Catholic church, since by law in 1832 all residents of Texas had to be Roman Catholics. Before the coffin was lowered into the shaft grave Bailey'd demanded, his wife placed in it his long rifle, a full horn of powder, his bullet bag full of bullets and flints, and his possibles bag loaded with a pipe, tobacco, a strike-a-light, and chaw.

Unfortunately, Mrs. Bailey was a member of a clandestine cold-water Methodist congregation that met secretly in and around the Brazoria area, and the preacher of the congregation, himself, was present at the funeral. In spite of Brit's wishes, she could not bring herself to put in his coffin the full jug of corn whiskey he'd demanded—especially not with that cold-water Methodist preacher looking on.

History records that Mrs. Bailey and her children abandoned the red house at Bailey's Prairie shortly afterward and moved to Harrisburg (now part of Houston). The house was rented to a succession of tenants, was eventually abandoned, fell into disrepair, and was torn down. Foundation stones—but little else—are supposed to remain on the site of Brit's sawlumber house, and the exact location of Brit's grave has been lost.

Where history leaves off, local legend takes over. It holds that the first family to move into the Bailey house left suddenly—as did all others. There was a reason for it. So the story goes, the first couple to live there practiced the most practical and effective form of early-19th-century birth control—separate bedrooms. About a week after they moved into the house, the wife suddenly came into her husband's bedroom—a "flying dive" might be the best way to describe her progress—and tucked her head under the covers in his bed.

"What's wrong with you, woman?" the husband asked.

"There was a man in my room," she wailed. "I thought it was you. He was on his hands and knees, feeling for something under the bed. I reached out to touch him—and my hand went right through him!"

The husband, to say the least, was skeptical, but his wife refused to spend the night in the room again. Finally he issued the ultimate challenge: "I'll sleep in there myself and prove there's nothing to it."

She apparently replied "Have at it, buster!"

Shortly after midnight a night or two later, he came out of the room at high speed. "Not only is there a man there," he said, "but I recognized him. It was old Brit Bailey himself."

Need we belabor the obvious? The bedroom in question had been Brit Bailey's, and, like any good frontiersman, he kept his jug under the bed.

For years afterwards, Brit Bailey manifested himself in various ways in and around Bailey's Prairie. His appearances became so well known that even the most skeptical believed whole-heartedly in the ghost at Bailey's Prairie. A visitor in the late 1930s reported that his car suddenly quit after dark at Bailey's Prairie, his radio came on without his touching it, the antenna went up and down, and his windshield wipers—which in those days operated off manifold pressure and wouldn't work at all unless the engine was running, and none too well even then—began to sweep back and forth across the windshield. The horn honked, the lights flashed—all without any apparent human aid—and finally, when everything stopped, the car could be started again.

Whether that's believeable to you or not, this part is a matter of historical record: an oil well being spudded in near the site of the old house collapsed in upon itself every time the bit was removed. When casing was placed in the hole the casing collapsed inward. There was no known physical reason for either the collapse of the hole or the collapse of the casing. No other wells in the area had behaved in that manner, and no fault was found in the casing pipes. When the well was moved some twenty feet, no further problems were experienced. Old-timers insisted that the well was being dug too close to Brit's grave, and he didn't appreciate it.

Brit has been dead some 158 years at this writing, the anniversary falling on Halloween of 1990. Of late his appearances have been limited to one every seven years. His last appearance was attested to in 1982. On Halloween of 1996 I hope to be at Bailey's Prairie with a bottle of the finest sour mash whiskey money can buy in tow. No matter how you look at it, for a man who appreciated good sour mash drinkin' whiskey to have to go 164 years without a snort is just too damn' long! I only hope Brit can still taste it.

SAM COLT, JACK HAYS, AND THE REPUBLIC OF TEXAS
- ONE HELLUVA PARTNERSHIP -

In 1986 Texas celebrated its Sesquicentennial of Independence. Just about the time most of us got to where we could pronounce sesquicentennial when sober, it was over. Three years later Texas had another sesquicentennial, but it wasn't well marked. It should have been. 1989 marked the sesquicentennial of the association of the international conglomerate known as Colt Industries and the Republic and State of Texas—an association without which there likely would have been no Colt Industries, and quite likely no Texas, either.

In the beginning there was Sam, and he brought forth the sixshooter, thereby making all men as equal as the Declaration of Independence said they were and the Constitution implied they were. That, at least, is the way the Gospel According To Colt reads. Unfortunately, it ain't quite so.

The idea of making a repeating firearm with a cylindrical magazine which rotated around a central axis was a very old one, dating back possibly as far as matchlocks. Both long guns and handguns with rotating magazines had been

made for several centuries before a young merchant seaman named Samuel Colt got in the game.

Arguably the best of the pre-Colt revolvers was
the Collier, a five-shot flintlock handgun made in
the 1790s. It had several problems, among them
an unfortunate tendency to let go all chambers at
once—a tendency it shared with a good many later
revolving pistols, some Colts included. The Collier
rotated its cylinder via a tightly wound coil spring,
which had several bad habits of its own. Besides
being unwound just when it needed to be wound,
the spring—if left wound up—tended to "set,"
freezing the cylinder in place with no impetus to
operate the repeating feature of the gun. If the
spring didn't set and the pistol was wound up
and ready to go, the spring-loaded detent, which
was supposed to allow the gun to skip to the
next chamber, sometimes let go and the cylinder
simply spun like a top until the thing unwound
when the weapon was cocked. The Collier was no
prize—more of an engineering toy than a serious
firearm—but it was a revolver, it did work part of
the time, and it preceded anything Sam Colt put
on the market by better than 45 years.

Sam Colt didn't invent the revolver, a century
and a half of Colt advertising to the contrary.
What he did invent was an improved system of
rotating and locking a revolver's cylinder which,
coupled with percussion-cap ignition—the system
most folks call "cap and ball"—made the first really
practical, dependable repeating handgun ever
sold. Sam, or so the story goes, was a 16-year-old
merchant sailor aboard an American trading ship
in the Indian Ocean when he took a hard look at
the ratchet system used to lock a ship's wheel in
place to hold the rudder in proper relation to the
set of the sails to maintain a set course at sea. He

said to himself, "What a jim-dandy way to make a repeating pistol."

Maybe so, maybe not. History does record that young Sam spent his seaman's pay, on his return to the U.S., for a nitrous-oxide generating outfit and, billing himself as "Dr. Coult," toured the Northeastern United States demonstrating the "wonder of the age," laughing gas. With the money he raised from his medicine show, he went into the firearms-manufacturing business, applying for his primary patent on a very significant day—February 23, 1836. It was the very day the siege of the Alamo began.

Colt began to manufacture a funny-looking, five-shot repeating pistol early in the fall of 1836. It wasn't a particularly good pistol, to be frank— more of a rich man's toy or an experiment in gunsmithing than a serious combat weapon. Originally, it had no integral ramrod or loading lever—it had to be taken to pieces to reload it, and the ramrod/loading tool was a separate and therefore potentially losable accessory. It had no triggerguard and no provision for one, which meant that it was hard to hold onto in a fight. It had no lanyard ring with which to tie the weapon to the man to eliminate loss in combat. Its trigger was a slim, delicate sprig of steel that broke off with distressing regularity.

By modern standards the gun was a joke, but a man with a brace or pair of these peculiar pistols had ten reasonably powerful, by the standards of the day, phenomenally accurate, shots in ten seconds or a little less. If he had a spare pair of cylinders and knew how to change them out quickly, in a little more than three-quarters of a minute he had ten more where those came from. Compared with a man who had a pair of one-shooter or double-barreled pistols that took roughly a half-minute per barrel to reload properly, the man with the repeater had a wonder weapon.

They say that if you build a better mousetrap the world will beat a path to your door, but don't you believe a word of it. Most likely, you'll wind up beating paths to the world's doors, trying to convince somebody—anybody—that your mousetrap really is better. That's what happened to Sam Colt. Sam really wasn't nearly the inventor he's gotten credit for being, but he—and his agents— were perhaps the most persistent salesmen who ever wore out shoe leather. They traveled all over what was then the United States, trying to peddle the revolutionary new pistol to the U.S. government, state militias, and anyone else who'd look and listen. They didn't have much success. In 1839 one of those agents came to the muddy streets of a frontier town that had just been named capital of a struggling republic—Austin, Texas. That, as it turned out, was both the stupidest and the smartest thing Colt ever did.

At the time Colt's agent arrived in Texas the republic was in the grip of several simultaneous crises, all of which, to one extent or another, involved money—there wasn't any. Sam Houston, who'd been president until 1838 but couldn't succeed himself, had managed, by scrimping, scraping, and saving, to establish a little credit for the new nation. Still, Texas really had nothing to offer anyone except perhaps land—most of which had title disputed with war arrows—and possibly western Gulf naval bases for European powers like France and Great Britain. Texas had lots of horses and cattle, neither of which as yet had great value outside the state, and no one knew about the oil or had a great deal of use for it if they did.

Mirabeau B. Lamar, who had great visions and absolutely no fiscal sense whatever, became president after Sam Houston, and he and Houston, for several reasons, cordially despised each other. The primary bone of contention between them was Indians—Sam liked 'em, particularly the Cherokees; Lamar considered the only good Indian a dead Indian and the sooner he got that way the better. In addition, the quartermaster general of the Republic of Texas was an ancient fossil named George Washington Hockley. Hockley believed that anything that didn't load from the business end and fire by flint and steel wasn't worthy of being called a gun. Into this mutual admiration society walked Sam Colt's representative, packing a suitcase full of the most revolutionary firearms ever offered for sale.

Lamar fell in love with the new guns on sight. So did Houston, which was a minor miracle—the two men could look at the same sundial at high noon and disagree on the time of day. Hockley, predictably, hated the whole idea. In a masterpiece of chicanery in which Lamar and Houston conspired to go over Hockley's head—or behind his back—Texas ordered 250 .40 caliber pistols and 100 .40 caliber revolving carbines.

There was only one minor hitch. The money to pay for them didn't exist. Hockley, who'd gotten wind of the deal, promptly spent the republic's entire arms budget for 1839 on an order of flintlock rifled muskets from Tryon of Philadelphia—guns which had been essentially obsolete for twenty years.

This didn't faze Lamar, who seems to have had all the monetary sense of a teenager turned loose with Daddy's American Express card. The president handled the negotiations himself, arguing that each weapon should have a spare cylinder and kit of tools included—he won that part of the argument—and finally agreeing that Colt could discount Texas paper money at four to one. The price, stated in U.S. dollars, would be paid with four Texas dollars for every U.S. dollar on the invoice.

A hundred pistols and 30 carbines had actually been delivered when Sam Colt realized how big a mistake he'd made. The Texas dollar had no backing whatever, and long before the contract was filled, those dollars Colt had agreed to accept at the equivalent of twenty-five cents U.S. had dropped to a trading value of around three and a half cents and would ultimately bottom out at two cents. In 1841 Colt's company, the Patent Repeating Firearms Company of Paterson, New Jersey, went flat broke. A lot of the reason for the bankruptcy, though neither Colt nor Texas historians like to mention it, was a stack of wastepaper called Republic of Texas dollars.

Lamar had intended for the 250 revolvers to be split, 50 to go to the Texas navy, 200 to arm the NCOs of his dream-world Republic of Texas Regular Army; the 100 carbines to go to the gloriously uniformed (at least on paper) Dragoon Regiment of the republic's regulars. This would have made—and did make, on paper—Texas's regular army the first formally organized national armed force on the face of the earth to be armed, officially, with repeating firearms.

There was, except in the president's head and on some planning papers, no Republic of Texas Regular Army. There was no money to pay one, and the land warrants issued for service in the regulars in lieu of money were valuable only when and if the Comanches were chased off the land. About a dozen of the pistols actually wound up with the much maligned Texas navy. The rest

went to the Indian-fighting militia known collec-
tively as "the Texian rangers." (It would be many
years before they became known as "Texas
Rangers," with capital letters.) Most of those
wound up in the hands of a company commanded
by a slim, grey-eyed Tennessean whom the
Comanche called, in literal translation, "Man-it-is-
very-bad-luck-to-get-in-a-fight-with-because-devil-
help-him." We know him better as John Coffee
Hays, Captain Jack Hays, or "Devil Jack."

The carbines were another story. They were
defective—weak in the cylinders—and Colt later
admitted this. The very first one ever fired blew
up in the hands of the soldier, and fragments of
the burst cylinder tore his forearm apart.
Gangrene set in and the man died. This gave
General Hockley a great opportunity to say "I told
you so," which he did not ignore. It was also worth
your life to suggest that anyone ever try to fire
another of "Colt's Patent Revolving Wheels of
Misfortune," as the carbines were promptly
dubbed. The 29 survivors were relegated to the
basement of something somewhere in Austin, and
generations of gun collectors have developed
"gold fever" over the possibility that 29 unfired—if
defective—1839-40 vintage Colt revolving carbines
might possibly still exist somewhere in the bowels
of Texas government. They aren't there, folks,
because God only knows how many folks have
looked to make sure over the years.

The combat debut of the Paterson revolver was
less than awe inspiring. In 1840, at the Council
House fight in San Antonio, an escaping
Comanche was pursued by a Paterson-armed
army officer. The officer drew his patented pistol,
drew a bead on the fleeing redskin, and let fly. The
gun not only didn't fire, the barrel fell off. The
officer tried again, and this time the cylinder fell

off. The enraged officer heaved the rest of the gun at the fleeing Comanche, jumped on his horse, rode his quarry down, and got him with a sword. The wedge which held the pistol together had worked loose in the holster.

The next time the Patersons saw combat they came off a little better. At Bandera Pass a party of about 25 rangers was bushwhacked by a war party numbering somewhere between 100 and 150 Comanches. The rangers were armed with flintlock and percussion long rifles and plains rifles—and two Patersons apiece, plus two preloaded spare cylinders each.

The Comanches caught the rangers by surprise and the white men, in true early-frontier style, dismounted with their backs to a rock ledge, downed their horses, and prepared for a mountain-man style battle. The Indians made a false charge to draw the fire of the deadly but slow-to-reload rifles, then charged in earnest, expecting to meet only ineffective short-range fire from one-and two-shot smoothbore pistols and to overwhelm the Texians in short order. It didn't quite work out that way.

With their rifles empty, the rangers drew their new, untried repeating pistols. The Comanches charged—and ran headlong into a regular hailstorm of hot lead. They pulled back and regrouped, and as they did so the rangers changed out their empty cylinders for fresh, fully loaded ones. The Comanches charged again—and met that same deadly blizzard of pistol balls. When the smoke cleared some 70 Comanches, including the war chief, were dead. The rest were headed for the tall and uncut, trying to get away from "guns that speak a time for every finger on a man's hand." The rangers themselves didn't lose a man, and the only reason any Comanches survived was ranger ignorance of what they had. The white men dismounted and let the fight come to them, which is a good tactic when your enemy has you outnumbered and outgunned, but a bad one when you're outnumbered but you have the enemy outgunned. Revolvers were really only adequate in defense. They worked best in the attack—as Jack Hays was shortly to prove.

Only a few months later, not that far west of Bandera Pass in present Kimball County, Hays and a party of 22 rangers were the object of a classic "Comanche wheel" attack by Comanches and Comancheros. This is the trick you've seen in the movies—the one where the Indians get the settlers or the soldiers or the wagon train or whatever in the middle of a circle, then ride round and round shooting until everybody in the middle of the ring is dead.

The Indians and renegades had the rangers outnumbered about six to one. Hays deliberately led his men into the trap and when it began to close—a situation that had almost always spelled death for those caught in the middle of the wheel—told his men "Powderburn 'em." The rangers pulled their new repeaters, took their reins in their teeth, and charged the closing ring. They smashed through, revolvers blazing, wheeled, and smashed into the would-be ambushers again.

Something on the order of two-thirds of the Comanches and renegades went down, the rangers lost two men, and Jack Hays had invented, on the spur of the moment, the tactics that would mark all successful use of repeating-handgun-armed light cavalry until the era ended with World War I—charge your enemy and shoot your way through, carrying the fight to him rather than waiting for him to bring it to you.

Please note very carefully what Hays told his men—"Powderburn 'em!" Shooting a handgun from the back of a galloping horse doesn't work like it did in the Roy Rogers movies. Hays' rangers charged in among the enemy, shooting at close range. Hitting anything but the ground—except by sheer accident—while shooting a revolver (or any other firearm) from the back of a galloping horse is nothing short of a miracle.

While the Paterson was being proved an excellent light-cavalry weapon in a mounted fight by his men, Jack Hays proved—not necessarily willingly—that it was a pretty fair item to have around in a man-to-man scrap as well. Hays was called, in the quaint Victorian phrase used to describe such people, "a man who does not know fear as others do." A Comanche chief put it more bluntly—"Devil Jack, him heap feller. Not scared to go to Hell all by himself." In the more expressive language of a later day, he could well be characterized as "a damned fool who doesn't have the good sense to be scared." Jack Hays had a reckless disregard for personal safety—his own, or anyone else's. It nearly got him killed one evening at a place called Enchanted Rock.

In 1841 Hays was guiding a party of surveyors near Enchanted Rock when he slipped off, as he often did, to do a little sightseeing on his own. Not far from the massive granite dome he was surprised by a small party of Comanches, who recognized the slim figure of "Devil Jack." They immediately set out to collect his celebrated scalp.

Hays was well mounted, and he outran the Indians to the rock. He rode his horse as far up the detritus of the dome's decay as he could, released the animal, grabbed his short plains rifle and his possibles bag, and climbed the rest of the way to the top up the slick, almost featureless pink granite. Modern climbers in grip-soled climbing shoes make that climb a careful step at a time. Hays made it on a dead run, in slick-soled boots— but then, he had more than average incentive.

In the top of Enchanted Rock there are a number of depressions, and Hays dropped into one of them overlooking the trail he'd taken to the top. The Comanches followed him, and as soon as the top of the first Indian's head showed over the curve of the dome, Devil Jack put a rifle ball through it.

There is something almighty daunting about seeing the leader of your band take a rifle ball between the eyes and roll head over heels down two hundred or so feet of slick rock. While the next Comanche got up the courage to peek over the curve of the dome, Hays stuffed his coat with grass—grass grows in the depressions atop Enchanted Rock—made himself a rest, and hauled out his Paterson repeaters. As soon as the next head was visible he put a hole in it, as well. The next time it was tried, two Comanches came up separately—and the gun-that-speaks-a-time-for-every-finger-on-a-man's-hand nailed both of them with two quick, accurate shots.

By this time the survey party had missed their guide, so they followed the sound of echoing gunfire to Enchanted Rock. The Comanches, trapped between a dozen or so deadly plains rifles behind and the equally deadly revolvers in front, died to a man.

The tale has grown until Devil Jack and his Paterson Colts wiped out a third or so of the Comanche nation in an all-day fight, but in truth the surveyors Hays was guiding saved the young, reckless ranger's bacon. The Colts were useful, but had reinforcements not showed up, the likelihood is very great that the setting sun would have seen

Jack Hays' sandy scalp decorating a war shield and some lucky Comanche in possession of a pair of "many-speak guns."

All of this, however, happened in Texas, and Texas was a long way from the big-money gun markets of the east. As far as Texas and Texians were concerned, Sam Colt's pistols, for all their many, many faults and shortcomings, were the best thing to come down the road since gunpowder. Texas news didn't spread very fast in the 1840s, though, and while Jack Hays was climbing down off Enchanted Rock—and probably kissing his pistols in the process—Sam Colt was going painfully broke. The Patent Repeating Firearms Company went into receivership in 1841. The assets of the company, including just about everything but Sam's patents, were sold at auction. Sam Colt, firearms innovator and salesman supreme, went to work for the Eli Whitney manufacturing conglomerate—Whitney made everything from plow points to rifles—and learned a lot about mass production.

Paterson revolvers were never very plentiful in Texas—there were probably less than 200 of them in the entire republic: 100 or so in the hands of the rangers and perhaps that many again privately purchased—and only a few thousand were made in the short history of the company. Only the "Texian ranger" revolvers got a real wringing out under combat conditions, and they proved altogether too complicated and delicate for a soldier's working pistol. The supply of spare parts ran out and the frontier gunsmiths made do and simplified, sometimes cannibalizing broken guns for parts, other times simply rebuilding the guns' actions to make them simpler and more rugged. By the time Texas joined the Union in 1846, there were only about 50 working Patersons remaining in ranger service.

The U.S. Army had rejected the Colt pistols—though a couple of companies of U.S. Regulars during the Seminole wars in Florida had been armed, experimentally, with Colt carbines, and a good many officers of both the army and navy had bought Colt pistols as personal sidearms—and in 1846 it wasn't about to change the policy, especially as Colt was out of business anyway. Sam Walker, a young Virginia-born Texian who'd been a prisoner at Mier and survived the Black Bean drawing, was now a captain in Jack Hays' regiment of mounted volunteers with Zachary Taylor's army. Walker really didn't care what the army thought about Colts—he'd used them, he knew how effective they were, and he wanted more Colts for his company of volunteers. He made loud noises to that effect, and Congress heard.

The upshot was a purchase of 1000 new Colt-made revolvers for Hays' entire regiment—a gun that has since become known as the Walker Colt. Sam Colt was suddenly back in business on a government contract—making that initial sale to Texas, which had been a major factor in his bankruptcy, the smartest as well as the stupidest thing he ever did. Colt's Patent Repeating Firearms Company, now Colt Industries, owed—and owes—its existence to Texas.

Sam Colt never forgot that debt, and neither—for a very long time—did Texas. The roll-engraved scene on the cylinders of Colt's Dragoon Revolvers, manufactured in the 1840s and 1850s, shows Texian rangers in an Indian fight—though unless you already knew that you'd have a hard time recognizing the U.S. Dragoon-uniformed men shown in the scene as rangers. Rangers didn't

have uniforms then and the Texas Rangers still
don't have uniforms today. The scene roll-
engraved on Colt's Model 1851 Navy Revolver
—perhaps the most widely distributed percussion
revolver in world history—shows the Texas navy in
battle.

Texas and Colt, for many, many years, were
almost synonymous. When Governor Richard
Coke reorganized the rangers in 1874, the pistols
he purchased for them were Colt's metallic-
cartridge Model 1873 single-action revolvers, and
the last governmental purchase of those same
guns—the famous Colt single-action revolver the
movies have made the "gun of the west"—as
recorded by Colt's own records, was by the San
Antonio Police Department in 1930. In 1933, when
Chief L. G. Phares organized the new Texas Highway Patrol, the guns he ordered for his men were
nickel-plated Colt New Service double-action
revolvers in .38 Special caliber. Even today the U.S.
government-issued M-16 rifles used by the Texas
National Guard bear the famous rearing horse
trademark of Colt. Colt and Texas have been
partners in defense for better than 150 years. It is
entirely possible, even likely, that without Texas,
Colt would not exist, and without Colt, Texas
would have died aborning. Which makes the
second of Texas' three sesquicentennials—the
third being the sesquicentennial of statehood in
1846—a date worth commemorating.

SPECIAL NOTE

The Paterson Colt—more properly the Patent
Repeating Firearms Company pistol, since the
name "Colt" appeared on it only in the patent
information and the celebrated "rearing horse"
trademark was not yet designed—was made in
several sizes and calibers, ranging from tiny .28

caliber pocket revolvers today called "baby Patersons" to the full-sized "belt and holster pistols" that came to Texas. In late 1840 and 1841 a "second model" Paterson was offered, with an integral loading lever like the one that appeared on the pistol now known as the Walker Colt. The only Patersons in the Texas Memorial Museum in Austin are a boxed pair of these later pistols, leading many to believe that the original "Texas Paterson" revolvers had loading levers.

The weapons were unnecessarily complicated —the modern term is, I think, "over-engineered"— and contained parts that proved later to be unnecessary. Like all percussion Colts save one, the Patersons were made in four basic pieces—the frame which held all the working parts, the cylinder, the barrel, and a steel wedge to hold the other three parts together. This three-piece construction caused most firearms "experts" of the day to consider the Colt badly constructed, and it was at least partly because of this construction that the Colt was rejected as a combat firearm by the United States.

Texans considered the three-piece construction an advantage. A man armed with a pair of Colt revolvers and a pair of spare, preloaded cylinders could fire up his loaded cylinders, knock the wedge out of the pistol with the hilt of his knife, stick the wedge in his mouth, pull the barrel off and stick it in his belt, put the fired cylinder in his pocket, drop a preloaded cylinder on the spindle and spin it to seat it, stick the barrel back on, put the wedge back in its hole and smack it with a knife-hilt to seat it, and have a completely reloaded pistol in less than 30 seconds—which is not much longer than it takes a modern police officer to reload his service revolver with ammo from his belt or cartridge drop-box.

WHO WAS THREE-LEGGED WILLIE?

Judge Robert McAlpin Williamson, one of Stephen F. Austin's first settlers, made a notable record as a jurist and circuit-court judge during the period of the republic and early statehood. Texas named a county for him, in fact—Williamson County, just north of Austin, county seat, Georgetown. It was there that I came to manhood while riding a coyote dun.

There is nothing in all the world quite so dull as reading a recital of a judge's official life—first he ruled on this case, then he ruled on that one. The fun is in finding what the person behind the reputation was like—and Three-Legged Willie was a real rounder. Although he's all but forgotten today, Robert McAlpin Williamson—known as Three-Legged Willie—was one of Texas' most colorful characters.

First off, how did a noted lawyer and judge get stuck with a nickname like "Three-Legged Willie?" Well, mostly because he had three legs—in a manner of speaking, anyway. He wasn't born with three legs, but as a child, back in North Carolina, he'd been struck with what was known as "white paralysis"—probably polio. The disease left his left leg withered and useless from the knee down.

Later in life Williamson attached a peg leg to his knee, folded the useless portion of his leg behind him, and had his clothes tailored with three legs—one for his good leg, one to cover his peg leg, and an extra tube on the left leg from the knee down to cover his useless shank. Amidst good leg, bad leg, peg leg, and walking stick, Williamson made a striking and odd sight. No one was more aware of it (or enjoyed it more) than Three-Legged Willie himself.

"I was awakened from a sound sleep," wrote Noah Smithwick in *Evolution of a State*, probably the best of the early-day Texas memoirs, "by a pounding upon my door."

The door-pounder was Williamson. "Look here, Smith," he yelled. "A man has broken his leg. Give a hand."

It was very late—or very early, depending upon from which end you prefer to overtake dawn—and Three-Legged Willie, more than a little worse for wear after an all-nighter with some friends, was walking home in San Felipe de Austin. He apparently hung his peg leg in a gopher hole and snapped it off. He then sought the aid of the only "doctor" who could help him—Noah Smithwick, San Felipe de Austin's blacksmith—to repair the damage.

Smithwick also relates the tale of Three-Legged Willie and the "pet buffalo" he didn't tame—something that could never have happened to a completely sober judge. Judge Williamson, then but a mere lawyer, encountered a lone, apparently orphaned buffalo calf and decided to catch the thing and make a pet of it.

This was not a just-born baby buffalo. It wasn't half-grown by any means, but it was big enough to take care of itself—and to make a sizable dent in a feller if he messed with it. Three-Legged Willie didn't just mess with it, he roped it.

What Willie wanted was a pet buffalo. What the buffalo wanted was no part of Williamson. Willie got off his horse to catch his pet-to-be. The buffalo promptly butted him and knocked him about six feet.

Willie got up, shook his head, dusted himself off, and began to approach the buffalo once more, speaking in a soft and soothing tone. The buffalo butted him again—several times.

By this time Willie realized that this buffalo, at least, wasn't going to make a pet anytime soon if ever, so he decided to take his rope off and just let the animal go. The buffalo, however, didn't interpret Williamson's peaceable intent properly. Not only that, it had discovered that butting this funny-looking three-legged critter was fun—it bounced, got up, and stood still where it could be butted again. The buffalo bounced Willie around three or four more times.

Willie got mad! He made it to his horse, mounted, and detached a heavy iron stirrup. He rode up close to the buffalo, fell off the horse onto the buffalo's back, and while the buffalo bawled, kicked, and bucked over several acres, he hung on for dear life with one hand and beat the beast on the head with the stirrup in the other until he killed it. Then he butchered it out on the spot and enjoyed buffalo-calf steaks for a while.

After Texas became a republic, Williamson became one of the first circuit-court judges. His circuit included Gonzales County.

Gonzales County, in those days, was a downright rough place. It didn't have much law of its own and it didn't want anybody else's law, either. For years Gonzales County refused even to build a courthouse—what court got held was held under the spreading branches of a liveoak tree.

Judge Robert McAlpin Williamson, Circuit Court Judge for the Republic of Texas, came to Gonzales County to hold court whether Gonzales County liked it or not. Gonzales County didn't make it any easier—the bar of justice was a rough plank laid across a couple of whiskey kegs under the oak, and the judge sat on a nailkeg.

Judge Williamson sat down, leaned his walking stick and long rifle against the oak tree, laid out his lawbook and gavel, and pronounced court in session. Gonzales decided to teach this upstart from Austin a lesson in how court was regarded in Gonzales County. The spectators got rowdy, and the more and louder the judge called for order in his court, the rowdier and louder they got. This might have intimidated some judges—but this was Three-Legged Willie.

The judge reached behind him, picked up his long rifle, laid it across the bench, cocked the hammer, and put his finger on the trigger. Things got very quiet very suddenly.

"This court," said Willie, "is coming to order. If it doesn't come to order—right now—I am by God gonna kill somebody, and I'm not particular who I kill." Court came to order in Gonzales County. Court always came to order in Gonzales County after that—especially when Judge Williamson presided.

They tell the tale of Three-Legged Willie and the drunken lawyer, and that's always worth retelling. The county isn't specified—it could have been any number—but the result is Texas legal-system legend.

The lawyer in question was arguing a civil case. He didn't have much of a case and was depending on his eloquence to carry the day. As his argument continued, he had frequent resort—for refreshment purposes—to a brown jug he kept at his table. The jug did nothing to clarify his reasoning or to strengthen his case, but it did wonders for his eloquence. The more often he refreshed himself, the more circuitous his reasoning became and the louder and more expansive he got.

Finally, Judge Williamson had enough. "Counselor," he demanded, "where is the law to support your contention in this matter?"

It's possible, I suppose, that the lawyer just didn't realize who he was dealing with—though in early Texas nearly everybody knew Three-Legged Willie by sight and reputation. It's also possible—and much more likely—that he forgot, in the heat of the moment and with the help of his jug, Judge Williamson's celebrated temper and reputation. He reached under his coat and produced a foot-long Bowie knife, which he waved at the judge. "This, by God," he announced, "is the law in this case."

Judge Williamson's hand went under his coat. When it came out it held a horsepistol with a bore big enough for a man to stick his thumb in. The hammer was back and Three-Legged Willie's finger was on the trigger.

"And this, by God," he said, "is the Constitution. You, sir, are overruled."

Judge Robert McAlpin Williamson left a legacy as a fair and honest judge. He left a legend as a man it just didn't do to mess with. Perhaps we could use another Three-Legged Willie—maybe several of them—on the benches of Texas courts today.

JIM BOWIE'S ELUSIVE KNIFE

There are, right now, probably a thousand entirely different scholarly opinions as to what Jim Bowie's celebrated "Bowie Knife" looked like, and each scholar who holds one can present a stack of references and photographs of various knives owned, or at least alleged to have been owned, by the celebrated frontiersman, James Bowie. For years we have believed, here in Texas, that we knew what a Bowie knife was—it was one heckuva big, long toadstabber with a wide, thick blade, and it was characterized by a "clip" or false edge—which was called, in early Texas, a "gut-tickler" —on the upper side of the blade. Yet there exist photographs of knives documented as having been, at one time or another, in the possession of James Bowie himself, that do not have this clip.

First off, how did Jim get this reputation as a knife fighter? The simple truth is, that except for some unsubstantiated legends that are also attached to earlier and later frontier figures, there is no record that Jim Bowie ever fought a duel of any kind—knife, sword, or pistol—with anyone, anywhere, ever. In Paul I. Wellman's *The Iron Mistress*, a marvelously well-written but largely fanciful biographical novel of Bowie, big Jim is credited with at least three duels—one on the

Vidalia sandbar near Natchez, Mississippi, one
with his leather britches nailed to a log at Jean
LaFitte's Galveston Island pirate hangout, and one
in a darkened room in New Orleans.

The truth is, Jim—at least by historical evidence
—never got into but one duel in his life—the one on
the Vidalia sandbar—and he wasn't one of the prin-
cipals in that one. The original duel was between
a Marylander named General Montford Wells and
a Virginian named Dr. Maddox. Jim Bowie, according to a statement given by his brother Rezin
P Bowie (please note that there is no period after
the P—Papa Bowie was Reason Pleasaunts Bowie
and he named his second-eldest son Rezin P Bowie
Jr and didn't use any periods anywhere), had been
engaged to Miss Cecelia Wells, General Wells'
sister, but she died of pneumonia two weeks
before the scheduled wedding.

The fight, which was a general scrap involving
everybody handy, started after General Wells and
Dr. Maddox shot at each other, missed, and shook
hands. It started out as pretty one-sided. The Wells
party included General Wells, Samuel Cuny, and
Jim Bowie. The other side included Dr. Maddox, a
Colonel Crain, Major Morris Wright, and a man
named Blanchard. After Wells and Maddox shook
hands, Crain said to Bowie "I reckon it's time we
settled our differences" or something to that effect. He pulled pistols and shot Cuny down in cold
blood, then shot and wounded Jim Bowie. Crain,
Maddox, Blanchard, and Wright all attacked the
wounded Bowie, and Wright severely wounded
him again with a sword-cane.

This apparently really made Jim mad. When
the sand quit flying Cuny was dead. Crain,
Maddox, and Blanchard were running for cover.
Wright had been opened up like a watermelon
with Jim Bowie's knife. Bowie himself was

severely wounded twice and was expected to die. General Wells doesn't seem to have gotten hurt.

The knife Jim used in that fight was, by the statement of Rezin P Bowie, one he'd had made by Jesse Cliffe, a white man employed by the Bowies as a blacksmith on one of their Louisiana plantations, from an old file. It had, by Rezin's statement, a nine and one-quarter inch blade one and one-half inches wide, with a single edge from point to guard.

Whichever one it was, it certainly wasn't the knife Texas later came to know as "The Bowie Knife." It did, however, enjoy quite a vogue for a good while, and Rezin P Bowie employed a well-known knifemaker, a man named Searles, of Baton Rouge, Louisiana, to make a number of copies of it which he gave to friends. A good many of these Searles "Bowie knives" are still around, and they have an excellent claim to being "genuine Bowie knives" since they were made at the request of and presented by a genuine Bowie.

For many, many years it was believed that the "genuine Bowie knife" was made by an Arkansas blacksmith and cutler named James M. Black. Black himself stated that he made "the real Bowie knife" for Jim Bowie. According to Black's tale, Bowie heard of his expertise in knife-making—and Black was, in fact, a very good knifemaker—and came to him with a carved wooden pattern. This was a very common practice, and it would seem likely that the knife pattern Bowie brought was very much like the knife he'd used on the sandbar. So, said Black, he made the knife according to Bowie's pattern—and then made another knife, according to his own ideas of how a fighting knife should be made. Bowie, said Black, so admired the second knife that he paid $50 in gold for it. You could buy an ounce of bullion gold for $10 or so in the 1830s, which makes that fifty bucks a whopping price.

This story is the one, with some modification, that Wellman put in *The Iron Mistress* and is the one most folks consider the "true story of the origin of the Bowie knife." As more and more people research the Bowie knife, the story gets less and less likely. To begin with, Black didn't remember that he was the one who made the "real" Bowie knife until 1840. Jim had been dead four years and couldn't contradict him by then, and the "Bowie knife" business was booming. What better way to increase your knife-making trade than to claim—with perhaps some backing—that "If you want a real Bowie knife you come to me, 'cause I'm the feller what made the real one—the one Jim Bowie himself carried"? There are several more reasons that Black's claim is doubted these days, but that one will do for the moment.

Whenever and wherever—and by whomever—it was made, by about 1830 Jim Bowie was packing a whale of a knife, and it was the one that he brought to Texas and the one that became known as "The Bowie Knife." While we don't know exactly who made it or when or where it was made, we do know almost exactly what it looked like, and we've known that for quite a long time. We've known it because in 1834 James Bowie had ten "exact"—well, dimensionally identical, anyway—copies of his famous knife made, and he gave them to ten of his admirers/supporters.

The maker of the knives was Texas' writin' blacksmith, Noah Smithwick. In *Evolution of a State*, Smithwick states that Bowie brought him the original knife and had him make a pattern from it and then commissioned him to make ten copies of the knife. He did so, Bowie paid for them, and the fact that Smithwick had actually seen and held "The Bowie Knife" became well known—so well known that, in his own words, "I developed a substantial business in the making of such knives in various sizes."

Now, we don't know for sure precisely which of his many knives Jim had Smithwick copy, but we do know that it was a knife he was right proud of. If it hadn't been, he wouldn't have had Smithwick copy it. We also know that it was the knife Texas would recognize in 1834 as "The Bowie Knife"—a pretty fair copy of the knife Jim Bowie himself actually carried, because Jim Bowie himself was still around and kicking in 1834, and that knife was plainly visible in his belt. The knife Smithwick copied, then, was the knife Texas in general and Jim Bowie in particular considered "The Bowie Knife" in 1834-1836. If Smithwick's copies had not been faithful to the original, it is very unlikely that James Bowie would have accepted and paid for them.

Several of the original Smithwick Bowies are still around, in very high-priced private collections. In the 1950s one of them—possibly the Smithwick/Juan Seguin Bowie—was in the possession of a collector named John R. Norris, who lived on Castle Hill Drive in Austin. In 1953, in the one-room house made of heavy logs in which Mr. Norris housed his collection—including things like two Walker Colts, one of the celebrated "Branding-iron Pair" of Colt Single Action Armies with ribs fitted to the barrels, silver-plated and engraved with over 100 Texas cattle brands (he later acquired the other one as well) and God-only-knows what else—I was permitted to examine and measure that knife.

The Smithwick Bowie in Mr. Norris' possession had a blade ten and one-half inches long, two inches wide, and a quarter-inch thick. The clip or "gut-tickler" was three inches long and perfectly straight, not dished. The point was at the center-line of the blade. It had neither fuller nor ricasso. Knife folks know that a fuller is the so-called "blood groove" in the blade, which has all sorts of fanciful explanations for existing. In fact it helps stiffen a blade, in exactly the same manner that a T-shaped bar of iron is stiffer than a flat bar. The ricasso is that little piece between the hilt and the blade that isn't sharpened and usually has the knife-maker's trademark on it.

It had a perfectly straight iron crossguard, a full tang, and a grip made of two pieces of light colored wood—possibly bois d' arc (Osage Orange or "Hossapple")—which was fastened with two large rivets. The blade was marked near the guard with a large spread eagle and N. SMITHWICK in capital letters in a semicircle over the eagle. The dimensions of the Smithwick Bowie are identical to the dimensions Wellman gave for the Bowie knife in *The Iron Mistress*, which leads me to believe that he probably saw and measured a Smithwick Bowie in the research for the book.

There are, today, a half-dozen "genuine copies of the original Bowie knife" being sold on the limited-edition collector's market—one of which is marked "J. Bowie" on the blade. The original of that knife is alleged to have James M. Black's mark on the blade. According to Bill Adams, a Bowie knife researcher and the proprietor of Atlanta Cutlery in Conyers, Georgia, it's a Mexican-made knife, probably of late 19th century vintage. Bill knows his knives—his business is making them and his hobby is collecting them, and sometimes, he says, it's very hard to tell what's business and what's hobby.

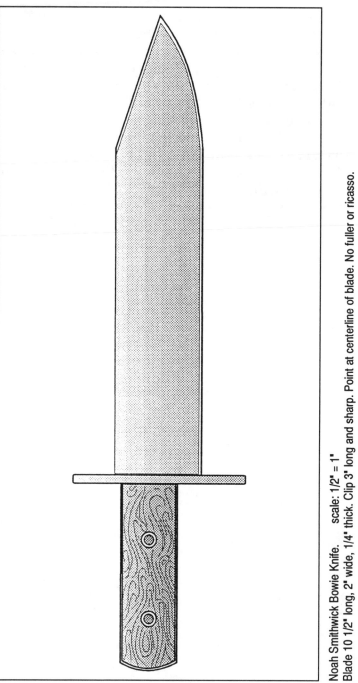

Noah Smithwick Bowie Knife.   scale: 1/2" = 1"
Blade 10 1/2" long, 2" wide, 1/4" thick. Clip 3" long and sharp. Point at centerline of blade. No fuller or ricasso.

While we don't know who made the original
Bowie knife for sure, or where or when it was
made, we do—thanks to Noah Smithwick—know
for absolute certain-sure what it looked like. In all
of the so-called "limited edition copies of the
original Bowie knife" I've yet seen, not even one
has come close to what I held in the log house Mr.
Norris had behind his main house on Castle Hill in
1953. For that reason, I haven't bought a "real copy
of the Bowie knife" from one of the reproduction
companies, and I don't intend to. You see, I know
what the real thing looked like, and they ain't it.

THE TREASURE OF
BRADY CREEK

I came by this tale in an odd way. In 1980, while doing research for *The Lost San Saba Mines*, I went to McCulloch County—Brady—to get as close as possible to the actual site of Jim Bowie's fight on Calf Creek. In exchange for some information and assistance from the *Brady Sentinel*, I agreed to write an article for the paper on the basics of treasure hunting.

I wrote the article, mailed it off, and went about the business of trying to get a book ready for publication. About a week later a lady called me at my home in Seguin. "Mr. Eckhardt," she said, "I have reason to believe that in 1835 James Bowie buried twenty-five jackloads of silver on my ranch. Would you be willing to try to find it for half the silver?"

You cannot—positively *can not*—jump through a telephone. I know. I tried.

The story the lady told me concerned an old black man who had once been the shoeshine man in a courthouse square barber shop in Brady. It has to start, though, with how the lady's ranch came to be.

McCulloch County is ranch country. It's limestone rock over granite, with very little dirt on top except in creek bottoms. It's cow, sheep, horse, or goat country. It definitely isn't country that's friendly to plows.

Sometime in the 1880s a promoter bought up the land on the banks of Brady and Bowie creeks, west of Brady, and sold it—sight unseen, mostly—to farmers. The farmers came, settled, tried to plow—and, predictably, went broke. The lady's granddaddy then made a business of buying the other feller's suckers out. He eventually acquired about 10,000 acres, some of which is presently under the waters of Brady Creek Reservoir.

After he'd gotten title to the land, the old shineman—then at least in his sixties and maybe older—came to him and asked his permission to dig along Brady Creek. Naturally, the owner wanted to know what the old man would be digging for.

The old man told a strange story. Back in 1835, he said, he and a cousin set out from San Antonio to walk to Austin to see some relatives. They got lost and eventually found themselves on the prairie north and west of where Brady now stands. They met a mule train of white men headed for San Antonio. The man in charge of the train was none other than the legendary James Bowie himself. Since they were lost, hungry, afoot in Indian country, and scared out of their wits, they asked Bowie if they could tag along to get back to San Antonio and home.

Bowie agreed. On the second night they camped along the banks of Brady Creek, at a place where some high white stone bluffs protected them from the north wind. The animals were unloaded and the party settled in for the night.

During the night Indians came and stole all the horses and mules. Come morning the party had to bury all their saddles and packs—which, the old man said, were loaded with bar silver—at the foot of the bluffs. They then started back to San Antonio, but the two boys got tired and decided to stop in Fredericksburg. The men went on, and they were all killed in the Alamo. That left the two young black boys the only people in the world who knew where the twenty-five jackloads of bar silver were buried.

As time went on the older boy died. The younger couldn't go back—McCulloch County was Injun country until the early 1870s, at least. Finally, when the Indians were all driven out and it was safe to go, the younger—now an old man— moved to Brady, got a job, and began to hunt for the silver. He wanted permission from the land-owner to continue.

This story has more holes, omissions, and downright lies in it than a political speech, but at bottom there seems to be a grain of truth. First off, black kids in 1835 were slaves. Slaves didn't go off "visiting relatives" seventy-five miles from home on their own.

There was no Austin in 1835, nor was there a Fredericksburg. Where Austin was established after the revolution there were two tiny villages— Waterloo, on the north bank of the Colorado, and Hornsby Bend, a few miles below Waterloo on the south bank. Fredericksburg wasn't founded until the mid-1840s. Nobody "going to Austin" winds up forty-five degrees and a hundred miles off course when there's really only one road that leads to Austin—and it was a pretty clear road—and no roads at all to where they wound up.

What really happened?

Most likely, two young slaves in San Antonio heard the Underground Railroad song that told them to "follow the drinkin' gourd to freedom" and headed toward the Big Dipper. Now, if you "followed the drinkin' gourd" and obeyed the other instructions in the song—and you were in the "old states"—you'd eventually find some of the Underground Railroad people, who'd hide you out, feed you, and smuggle you to the free states north of Mason and Dixon's line. If you "followed the drinkin' gourd" in Texas west of the Colorado, all it took you to was Comanches—and they weren't part of the Underground Railroad.

Jim Bowie certainly wasn't in present-day McCulloch County in 1835. He was in San Antonio de Bejar. Mostly, he was drunker'n a skunk in San Antonio de Bejar, and he'd been that way since his wife died. He hadn't been into the hills since November of 1831. His nickname may have been El Cuchillo Grande—the big knife—once, but by 1834 it was El Borracho Grande—the big drunk—and he stayed that way until about October of 1835, and we know for sure where he was after that.

What probably happened was this. The two kids took off for freedom's land, found Comanches instead, and were willing to trade freedom—and might near anything else—for a chance to get back to mamma with a whole scalp. They met—or were captured by—a group of white men who had a packtrain of mules. The leader wasn't Jim Bowie, but he had a big knife. He waved it at them and said, "I'm Jim Bowie, and if you give me any trouble I'll cut your gizzards out and eat 'em." They believed him.

They stopped at a place along Brady Creek where there were high limestone bluffs to break the north wind. The animals were put out on a picket line with a tallow-greased rawhide lariat. Sometime during the night a skunk or raccoon came and chewed the lariat in two, and the animals escaped. The white men told the boys "Injuns got 'em" and that made the children even more scared to run off. The loss of the animals required the men to bury the packs, which just might have contained silver and probably did.

The party set out southward, and somewhere along the line the men got tired of herding a couple of small black kids with them and either sold them or gave them to a homesteader northwest of San Antonio. Then the men went on to San Antonio. Some of them probably did die in the Alamo—maybe even all of them. There's no way to know.

The younger boy was in his forties by June 19, 1865—Freedom Day, when the Emancipation Proclamation was proclaimed in Texas—and the older one was dead. The hills north of San Antone were crawling with Indians. For perhaps thirty years more he hung on to the dream of twenty-five jackloads of silver, and finally, when it was safe to do so, he moved to Brady to try and find it.

He believed it was there. He got his permission, and from the late 1890s until he died in the early 1930s, he took every opportunity he could to dig and backfill holes all up and down Brady Creek. He never tried to cash in on his story, he never tried to sell shares in the silver, and he never begged a grubstake. He just worked until he could supply himself with food, packed his mule, and went up Brady Creek to dig. He was probably a hundred years old, maybe more, when he died— and he was still looking.

Now—were there once twenty-five jackloads of silver buried at the base of the limestone bluffs on the north bank of Brady Creek? I have no question that there were—at least for a while.

Were they still there when the old man went back to look for them? Maybe, but he sure didn't find them. There's no law that says all of those white men had to die in the Alamo. It's not impossible—nor is it unlikely—that sometime between 1836 and 1885 or so some or nearly all of those men returned to those high white bluffs, dug up that silver, and sold it in New Orleans.

No, I didn't find any silver either. My pal Mike Clemmer and I spent nearly a week running metal detectors and dowsing wires at the base of everything we could find that looked even remotely like "white stone cliffs" on the north bank of Brady Creek. The only thing that set the electronics to squealing were some old paintbuckets. But that doesn't mean that I didn't find The Treasure Of Brady Creek. I sure did—this story, once almost lost, now preserved. For a storyteller, a good story is often better than jackloads of silver.

JIM BOWIE AT CALF CREEK

Texas history has a lot of legend in it. That's a fact, and even the best historians can't deny it. Oh, they will, and they do—but if you can catch them over a pitcher of beer and their guard's down, they'll admit it. There's about as much legend in Texas history as there is history in Texas history.

We're not alone in this by any means. Folks have been trying to prove there was an historical King Arthur for longer than the United States has been a country, and they've been trying to prove there really was a Robin Hood for nearly as long as they've been trying to prove King Arthur. Whether or not there really was an Earl of Huntingdon named Robert Locksley who called himself Robin o' the Hood or Robin Hood—or whether or not there really was a Dux Brittanorum known as Artorius Arctos or Artos the Bear, who has become known as "King Arthur"—really doesn't matter much, though. The Arthurian Cycle is not merely one of the world's great tales, it's a pretty fair semihistorical account of the Brittano-Cymryc resistance to the Norse conquest of the British Isles after the Romans left. The tales of Robin Hood are, just about any way you take 'em, one helluva collection of hero stories of resistance against tyranny.

The written history of Texas is just short of five hundred years long. It really began, so far as we know, in 1519, when Alonso de Piñeda sailed down the Texas coast and christened every creek mouth and river mouth he saw after one saint or another. For slightly less than the next three centuries, most of Texas' history can be capsuled as a bunch of Spaniards and Frenchmen looking, on alternate moonlit Thursdays, for the mouth of the Mississippi River, a lot of gold and silver, and each other to shoot at. For the first two centuries of that period, that was about all that was going on.

Well, they didn't find the mouth of the Mississippi—mostly because it never has had one; it has a delta like the Nile. They didn't find much gold and silver but they found a helluva lot of space to look for it in. They managed to find one another and burn a little powder on a rough average of about once every half-century or so.

The real history of Texas didn't begin until the early 1700s, when San Antonio was founded. From that time to the present, there have been—present and writing—people who could not only read and write but were determined to record, as closely as possible, what was happening.

Compared to a lot of places—Europe in particular—Texas hasn't really got all that much history. How did we manage to mix so much myth into it? We really didn't need to, you know. I'm not all that old—though I'm older than I care to admit in the presence of younger women—and I can remember men and women, from my boyhood, whose fathers and mothers had known Jim Bowie, Buck Travis, and Stephen F. Austin by their first names. I knew men and women who, as youngsters, had known Robert E. Lee and Sam Houston—not to mention John Wesley Hardin, Sam Bass, and Ben Thompson.

We can blame Hollywood and the movies for a lot of it, and it does deserve a lot of the blame. The very first movie ever made about the Alamo was made by a Frenchman named Georges Meliere. It was about nine or ten minutes long, and Meliere himself played Davy Crockett. The second movie made about the Alamo, *Heroes of the Alamo*, was made by David Wark Griffith—the same D. W. Griffith who made *Birth of a Nation*—and it was made in the United States. Well, maybe it wasn't really Griffith himself—maybe it was one of his second-unit directors. Anyway, it wasn't anywhere near the hit *Birth of a Nation* was. It got lost somehow and stayed lost for something like sixty-five years—except for a few stills and some short clips—and it wasn't until the 1980s that the entire movie was found, pieced together, and shown. That's when we found out how really bad it was.

Among other things, *Heroes of the Alamo*, had "Sam Houston's trusted scout, 'Silent' Smith" (apparently somebody didn't hear right when they were told Erastus Smith was called "Deaf Smith" because he had a hard time hearing a gun in his ear), trying to do in one of Santa Anna's soldiers with an English-made Tranter double-action revolver, which didn't exist until about forty years after San Jacinto. It also had, at the climactic battle on the plain of St. Hyacinth, the Texas army advancing upon the Mexican lines, carrying tumbleweeds for camouflage. This scene may have been an adaptation of a scene from Shakespeare's *MacBeth* where MacDuff's men carried fronds cut from Birnam Wood above their heads as they sneaked up on Dunsinane Castle. Forget the fact that San Jacinto is in a swamp and tumbleweeds grow on the high plains. There weren't any tumbleweeds—none at all—anywhere in the United States until the 1880s, when a group of Mennonite farmers immigrated from the Russian steppes and carried, hidden in their clothing, seeds for Russia's famed hard-hulled, winter-hardy wheat. Among them they carried the almost microscopically small seeds of Amaranthus Graecizans—the plant we call the "tumbleweed."

For the record, *Birth of a Nation* wasn't a bit more historically accurate than Griffith's Texas movie. One of the old Daughters of the Confederacy told me, years ago, that she took her daddy, an Army of Northern Virginia veteran, to see it when it first came out. When the "boy colonel" charged the Yankee lines and rammed the staff of the battleflag into the bore of the Yankee cannon, he walked out. He said things to the effect that the last time he'd seen that many roadapples in one place was right after Jeb Stuart's cavalry passed.

One of the better—and most thoroughly mythologized—Texas tales is the story of Jim Bowie's fight with the Indians at Calf Creek, in what is now McCulloch County, in 1831. The fight involved a number of names well known in Texas history: James Bowie, his brother Rezin P Bowie Jr, Cephas (or Caiphas) K. Ham (or Hamm), and James Coryell (Coryell County is named for him), and some not so well known today, like Thomas McCaslin and Matthew A. Doyal. Most accounts of the battle are based on the accounts left by Rezin P Bowie and Cephas Ham, and they contain far more myth than fact—and always have. Since the first telling, the myths have grown, and I recall being told over a Llano County campfire that "how come ol' Jim Bowie 'n' 'em, 'ey whupped all 'em Injuns up on Ca'f Creek; ol' Bowie 'n' 'em, 'ey had sixshooters 'n' Winchesters 'n' all 'em Injuns had wuz bows 'n' arrers 'n' 'em ole frontloadin' guns whut jes' shoot one tahm."

The battle at Calf Creek took place in late November of 1831. Sam Colt didn't even apply for his first patent on a repeating pistol with a rotating magazine until February 23, 1836—the day the Alamo siege began. The first production weapons from Patent Repeating Firearms Company of Paterson, New Jersey—the guns we call "Paterson Colts" today—didn't appear until September of '36. They shot five times, not six. The first Colt sixgun, the First Model Dragoon Revolver, more popularly known as the Walker Colt or the Whitneyville Dragoon Revolver, didn't make an appearance until late 1846. The first American lever-action magazine rifles, the Volcanics, designed by B. Tyler Henry and Daniel B. Wesson, made their debut in 1854. The first American metallic-cartridge repeating rifle, the Spencer, first came out in 1858. B. Tyler Henry's first cartridge gun—the Volcanic used ammunition in which the bullet was its own cartridge case—appeared in 1862. The first Henry-designed rifle with the name Winchester on it appeared in 1866. The Battle of Calf Creek, then, preceded Colts of any sort by five years, Colt sixshooters by fifteen years, lever-action magazine rifles of any sort by better than twenty years, and Winchesters by a solid third of a century. All anybody at Calf Creek had was "bows 'n' arrers 'n' 'em ole frontloadin' guns whut jes' shoot one tahm."

The generally accepted version of the Calf Creek fight—and the one you'll find in standard histories (when you can find it at all, which isn't often)—is pieced together from accounts given by Rezin P Bowie and Cephas Ham. On November 2, 1831 Jim Bowie, his elder brother Rezin, and a party of anywhere from seven to twenty-three white men, depending on who's doing the telling at the time, left San Antonio to go into the

red-granite hills to the north. They were search-
ing—or so they said—for the already-legendary Los
Almagres silver mine, supposed to have been
"lost" for many years. Today that "lost mine" is
better known as the Lost Jim Bowie Mine or the
Lost San Saba Mine.

As we follow the story, we find that the group
actually found the mine, that they entered it, and—
according to Rezin P Bowie—they found therein a
vast vein of almost pure silver, from which they
cut chunks with their sheath knives and
tomahawks. They loaded this raw—but better-
than-coin-pure—silver on their mules and started
back to San Antonio as rich men.

Late in the afternoon of November 19, somewhere along the San Saba River tributary known
as Calf Creek, they were overtaken by a "friendly
Comanche." (Yes, there really were such things as
"friendly Comanches" in 1831—at least some
Comanches were friendly to some white men
some of the time.) The Comanche warned them
that they were being followed by a large war party.

The makeup of the party seems to be a matter
for dispute among authors. Paul I. Wellman, in
The Iron Mistress, made them Lipans under the
command of Tres Manos, the warrior Bowie had
humiliated when he "lived with the Lipan."
Another authority says they were Apaches, while
another says they were Comanches. William H.
Fear—at least that's the name he used at the time—
a British writer of "six-shots-ahead-of-the-sheriff"
type westerns (and a feller who apparently chewed
up and swallowed *Coronado's Children* without
taking a drink of water), insisted they were
Caddos. Mostly, they're identified as a band of
Wacos and Tawakonis, and that's most likely what
they actually were.

Apparently the Indians were a ways behind, because Bowie and his party traveled until the afternoon of the 20th, then made camp on the north bank of Calf Creek near a large spring. They "fortified" their camp by dragging up brush and fallen trees and by upending the big, flat limestone slabs that covered the ground.

At first light on the 21st, the Indians attacked. According to Rezin P Bowie's account, there were exactly 164 of them. The Bowie party dropped down behind their improvised breastworks and—again according to Rezin P—the Indians attacked en masse time and again, only to be repulsed by the withering rifle fire from "Bowie's fort." When the sun set, the ground was littered with red-skinned corpses and gore—Bowie claimed fifty dead and thirty-four wounded, and you have to wonder who was idiot enough to stick his head up in the line of fire long enough to make the count. The "intrepid frontiersmen" lost one killed—Thomas McCaslin—and three wounded.

Except for the stone gateposts and some wall footings, what stands of Presidio San Luis de las Amarillas/Real Presidio de San Saba at Menard is entirely reproduction, built by WPA/CCC labor for the 1936 Centennial. Built primarily of rubble (uncut stone) and inferior cement and only sporadically maintained for the last half-century, today it is in a state of collapse.

The "Bowie Mine" inscription on the south gatepost of the Presidio is entirely fake. It dates from about 1905-1910. The original "Bowie" inscription on the gatepost, long since obliterated, read "Bowie con su tropa 1829." (The blackening of the inscription with a pencil is a recent addition.)

IN THIS VICINITY

ON NOVEMBER 21, 1831 JAMES BOWIE, REZIN
P. BOWIE, DAVID BUCHANAN, CEPHAS D.
HAMM, MATTHEW DOYLE, JESSE WALLACE,
THOMAS M^cCASLIN, ROBERT ARMSTRONG,
JAMES CORYELL WITH TWO SERVANTS,
CHARLES AND GONZALES, HELD AT BAY
FOR A DAY AND A NIGHT, 164 CADDOS
AND LIPANS • AFTER 80 WARRIORS HAD
BEEN KILLED, THE INDIANS WITHDREW

Erected by the State of Texas
1936

Considering that the inscription on this 1936-vintage historical marker contains only three minor errors of known fact, two probable errors of fact, and one glaring omission, it is one of the more historically accurate of the early markers. Rezin P Bowie's middle initial never took a period; Cephas Hamm's middle initial was K, not D; and Matthew Doyal's last name is misspelled. It is far more likely that the related and allied Wacos and Tawakonis were the Indian coalition at Calf Creek than the Lipans (an Apache band from below San Antonio) and the Caddos (a woodland tribe from deep East Texas). More like 15 or 20 Indians were killed, and the monument does not tell us that Thomas McCaslin was killed and Matthew Doyal severely wounded.

(1.3 miles north of Calf Creek on FM 1131, McCulloch County.)

Excuse me, folks, but this never happened. It could not possibly have happened, not as described, anyway. There was a battle like that, and it did have the results Bowie described—but it took place not on November 21, 1831, in the granite hills of Central Texas, but started on September 17, 1868, and lasted until September 25. It took place on a sandspit today called Beecher's Island, in the Arickaree Fork of the Republican River, in Colorado just south of where Kansas and Nebraska join on the Colorado line. The Indians were 700 Ogalala Sioux and Cheyenne Dog Soldiers, and the white men were "fifty first-class, hardy frontiersmen" commanded by Major George A. Forsyth of the U.S. Army.

The "hardy frontiersmen" were armed with seven-shot Spencer repeating carbines and each man had anywhere from one to four Colt or Remington sixguns for backup. Those sixguns, being essentially muzzle-loaders themselves, were slow to reload—but the Spencers weren't. A good rifleman equipped with a Spencer could put seven pretty darn accurate shots out in a half minute or so, reload with his "Blakeslee-patent reloading device" in about 35 seconds, and then do it again. He could keep doing it until the Spencer heated up to the point that it would cook off shells when he chambered 'em, at which time he'd either dip it in the creek or urinate on it to cool it and go back to shooting. He could keep doing it without interruption until the thing went down with one of the myriad malfunctions to which the Spencer was subject and he had to pull out his pocket knife and fix it.

The battle at Beecher's Island was fought so fiercely and at such close quarters that the men were often using their knives on Indians who made it into their improvised breastworks; the firing was so fast and furious that at times men were simply firing blindly into the thick cloud of powder smoke, knowing the Indians were so thickly packed that it would take a miracle to miss one. When it was finally over, six of the white men were dead, fifteen were wounded severely enough to require hospital treatment, and every member of Forsyth's party had sustained at least one minor wound. The Major estimated that in eight days of fighting they had actually killed thirty-five Indians and wounded about a hundred. Yes, there was such a fight as Rezin P Bowie described—but it didn't happen on Calf Creek in November of 1831.

Most of the rifles at Calf Creek, if not all of 'em, were flintlocks—and for good reason. The percussion cap had been around a while, but stores selling them were sort of scarce on the Texas frontier. If a feller shot up all his caps—or lost 'em, or accidentally got grease on 'em and "killed" the priming mixture—he was just up that famous creek until he could get some more caps. A man with a flint gun could pick up a chunk of flint, chert, or agate—and there's practically no place in Texas that you can't find chunks of flint, chert, or agate under your boots if you look hard—and, if he was any kind of a frontiersman at all, chip out a gunflint that would work for a few shots, anyway. It wasn't all that uncommon, even late into the 1860s, to see a frontiersman, packing a pair of Colt's cap-and-ball sixshooters on his belt, who stuck with his trusty flintlock rifle-gun for that very reason.

A man armed with a flintlock plains rifle, if he uses premeasured powder charges, pregreased patches, balls prepositioned in their patches in a loading block (and an unbreakable ramrod)—assuming he's very experienced in loading and firing such rifles and very familiar with the

particular rifle he'll be using (and he has a whole
possibles bag crammed full of four-leaf-clovers
and rabbits' feet and they work)—can start with a
loaded rifle and get off three aimed shots in 80 to
90 seconds. This presupposes ideal conditions.
The feller is standing up to do it. He has everything
neatly laid out in order on a flat surface at waist
height where he can grab it, he doesn't drop anything important, his flint doesn't come loose,
and—most important of all—nobody's trying their
dead-level best to blow his brains out while he
does it. Lying on your belly in the rocks and grama
or kneeling behind an upturned rock, shooting
over or around a fallen tree, rolling on your back
to reload with loose powder and ball, then rolling
back to shoot, while a whole bunch of very hostile
folks are doing their best to make great big bloody
holes in your hide so they can lift your hair afterwards, and war arrows and .75 caliber musket
balls are whistling over your head or plunking
into the rock in front of you, just doesn't qualify as
"ideal conditions."

There are almost as many "accurate counts" of
the number of frontiersmen in the fight as there
are tellers of the tale. The state historical monument records nine names plus "a Mexican
servant." Another tale says 14 white men and
Bowie's black servant, a man named Charles. One
account gives the total as 25 frontiersmen. The
number of Indians ranges from Rezin Bowie's 164
down to 90 and up to 250.

Let's try to reconstruct the fight as Bowie
described it, giving the frontiersmen the best
advantage they could possibly have had within
Bowie's account. We have 25 "seasoned Indian
fighters"—that's about ten more than Bowie
claimed—and 164 Indians. There would have been
Indians to watch the horses and, of course, the

medicine man, who accompanied every war party, took no active part in the fighting himself. That puts about 150 Indians for the initial attack.

To oppose them we have 25 men, each armed with a one-shooter rifle that it's gonna take about 30 seconds to reload once he's fired it and probably one or two one-shooter flint or percussion pistols, plus a tomahawk and a knife. The Indians begin their charge at 100 yards—it takes them about 20 seconds to make it to the breastworks. Each white man fires all three of his available shots—one rifle and two pistols—no weapon misfires, everybody hits what he shoots at every time and every hit is a fatal one, and no two men shoot at the same Indian. Now what have we got?

There are 75 unwounded, extremely angry Indians going bite-his-ear-off-and-kick-him-in-the-crotch-while-you-slash-his-throat with 25 white men, and there are at least 13 more Indians out there who can pitch in if things start going bad for their side. That's three Indians apiece plus reinforcements—and that's also about two Indians apiece too many for anybody, even Jim Bowie. Sure, Bowie took nine down with him in the Alamo, but they weren't enraged Indian warriors. They had to come through a narrow door one at a time to get at him, and as long as he held the door they couldn't get behind him. There were no such conditions at Calf Creek.

James Bowie and his men came out of that fight with four casualties—one killed, three wounded. That's a matter of indisputable historic record. How?

Matthew A. Doyal, who was there, told two tales of the Calf Creek fight. The one he told for public consumption pretty well paralleled the Bowie and Ham versions. The one he told at home in front of the fireplace to his children and grandchildren differed markedly from "accepted history." I got this tale from Matt's grandson, Ralph A. Doyal, who got it straight from his granddaddy, who was there. This is the way Ralph told it.

There really wasn't all that much of a fight at Calf Creek, at all. Members of Bowie's party, James Coryell, Rezin P Bowie, and Cephas Ham were about as fine a trio of riflemen as Texas could boast in 1831. The Indian war party made medicine and then got together to rush the breastworks. One of the braves stood up and yelled the equivalent of "All right, boys—let's go get 'em!" One of the riflemen promptly sent him backside over elbows into the weeds with a rifle-ball in his gizzard. This had a sort of dampening effect on the immediate enthusiasm of everybody else. The medicine man made more medicine; somebody else stood up and hollered—and did a backflip with a half-inch hole through his totem paint. If you keep this sort of thing up long enough, sooner or later you're going to run shy on folks fool enough to stand up and holler. Since the classic approach hadn't worked, the Indians decided to try something else. They began to crawl through the tall grass, one at a time, inching up close enough to get a quick shot with a trade musket or a bow. A good many of them never got that close. When you crawl through grass, you disturb not merely the grass but the critters in it. There are still flies and grasshoppers out in November in Central Texas, and a grasshopper suddenly jumping up or an eruption of flies from the grass means something is moving through it—right where the flies or the grasshopper came up from. Every such sign brought a rifle-ball, and while some of the Texans undoubtedly missed altogether or hit some poor benighted critter that was only trying to catch a grasshopper for dinner, some of them undoubtedly hit crawling Indians.

Some of them made it, though. One Indian in particular managed to blindside the "fort," poked a huge trade musket through the brush, and let fly. The first shot hit James Buchanan in the shin. The second hit Matt Doyal in the chest. The third time they saw the muzzle come through. One man grabbed the barrel and shoved down—hard. The astonished warrior on the other end popped up— and found that he was looking a buckshot-loaded horsepistol square in the eye. It was the last thing he ever saw.

There is a story about the fight that may or may not be true, but it belongs in a book of stories anyway. If you've ever breathed black powder smoke, you know it makes you powerfully thirsty. According to the story, Jim Bowie gave his black servant, Charles, a bucket and told him to run to the spring below the fort and bring back water. Charles didn't want to go—there were Indians out there. Bowie pulled that big knife and said, "If you go, the Indians might kill you. If you don't go, I will kill you." Charles went for the water.

What happened after Matt Doyal was hit we can't be too sure about, because our informant was understandably preoccupied—he had a three-quarter-inch hole in his chest. We do know that the frontiersmen had no medical supplies of any kind, so that night they "boiled some liveoak bark very strong, thickened it with powdered charcoal and Indian meal, made a poultice of it . . . " and fastened it to Buchanan's leg with a bandage of sewn-on buffalo hide. Doyal's wound—and a third wounded man in the party—probably got similar treatment.

Now, about that silver. According to Matt, there wasn't a silver mine. Jim Bowie's "silver mine"

had legs. Mexican silver was transported overland
by mule train from mines deep in Sonora, crossed
the Rio Grande at Presidio del Norte (now
Presidio, Texas), followed the spring line north of
Paisano Pass, crossed the Pecos at Horsehead
Crossing, turned northeast through Castle Gap to
catch the Middle Concho about as far as present
San Angelo, and then turned south to catch the
water of the San Saba, Llano, and Pedernales
rivers down to San Antonio. From San Antonio
they followed the Camino Real to Louisiana and
then boated the silver down the Red and Mississippi rivers, where in New Orleans it was traded
for letters of credit that would allow Mexico to
make overseas purchases. Bowie, as the son-in-law
of the vice governor, had inside information on
when the silver trains would come through and
what their routes would be, and he "mined" silver
by the simple expedient of snatching the last two
or three mules off the trains.

There is at least some historical reason to
suppose this might be true. Before the siege closed
in on the Alamo, Bowie and a small party were out
scouting and spotted a Mexican mule train. Those
mules, Bowie told his men, carried enough silver
to buy anything and everything Texas needed. The
party attacked—and grabbed a mule train loaded
with prairie hay, cut for Santa Anna's cavalry
horses. We call this, in Texas history, "the Grass
Fight."

Now why would Jim Bowie think those mules
were loaded with silver? Why, indeed—unless he'd
previously taken pack mules from the Mexicans
and they *had* been loaded with silver?

According to Doyal, the silver Bowie and his
men had—which amounted to three mule loads at
300 pounds per mule, or 900 pounds of bar silver—
was buried either in or very near the improvised

"fort" in a hole "waist deep on a tall man." In the hole, as well, were put a knife described as a "bowie" and a tomahawk. Thomas McCaslin was buried near the "fort," and the men—now afoot, for the Indians had taken all the horses and mules —made stretchers from saplings and coats and carried Doyal, Buchanan, and a third man to the community now known as Camp San Saba. The men agreed that no one man would ever go back to dig up the silver alone—only all the party together would do so.

In the spring of 1833 Señora Ursula María de Veramendi Bowie, along with James Bowie's only known child, died of yellow fever. Jim took a headlong dive into a whiskey jug and stayed in it until 1835. So far as anyone knows for sure, he never returned to the granite hills. So far as anyone can say for sure, 900 pounds of bar silver still rest in a hole "waist deep on a tall man" somewhere along the banks of Calf Creek.

OIL!

The foundation stone of Texas' twentieth century economy since the century dawned has been a dirty-black, greasy, foul-smelling substance called "oil"—raw or "crude" petroleum. Yet it almost wasn't—or at least it almost wasn't the foundation of a private-ownership economy.

Oil has, of course, been around almost forever, but for most of human prehistory and history its uses were extremely limited. Natural petroleum seeps—called "oil springs"—existed all over South and East Texas, and Indians used the tarry residue found around the seeps as a medicinal salve or for waterproofing baskets and canoes. White settlers later used the same stuff—they called it "bitumen"—to aid in chinking the walls of their homes, for waterproofing things, and, like the Indians, as a medicinal salve. It was highly recommended as a salve for saddle galls or harness galls on horses.

This residue—a soft, sticky, smelly tar-like substance—was what remained in and around the oil spring when the hot Texas sun evaporated the more volatile components of the oil. The "tar balls" that appeared on Padre Island's beaches a few years ago—and caused ecological panic—were this same stuff. They weren't anything new to Padre Island, either, or to any other Texas Gulf

Coast area, though it had been a while since they
were last seen there.

South and East Texas, for centuries, literally
floated on a vast reservoir of oil. When oil was
discovered around Houston and massive pumping began, in many places—the San Jacinto
battlefield being the most immediately noticeable—the ground literally dropped several feet in
elevation. In 1836 the San Jacinto battlefield was a
raised prairie between two sluggish creeks. By
1936 it was low-lying swampland flooded by those
same creeks. When the oil was pumped out from
under it, the ground sank about ten feet.

For thousands of years, about 100 miles off the
Texas coast, there was a massive natural oil seep
that spread a permanent oil slick over hundreds of
square miles of the Gulf of Mexico. This oil slick
was well known to ships' captains plying Gulf
waters and was marked on navigation charts right
up into the twentieth century. In storms, ships
sought out the oil slick, because the oil on the
waters kept the Gulf somewhat calm there, even in
heavy weather. This natural oil slick, which had
been a fixture of Gulf of Mexico ecology for millennia, disappeared in the 1920s after massive
on-shore pumping artificially relieved the natural
underground pressure that forced the oil upwards.

Tar balls—the gooey residue from the natural
oil slick—were also a fixture of Gulf Coast ecology
for thousands of years. Coastal Indians gathered
them for use in waterproofing their basketry and
boats. Fragments of hardened tar with the intri-
cate patterns of the perishable basketry impressed
in them have been a common archaeological find
along Texas' coast ever since there has been
archaeology there. It is from these tarry remnants
that we know the Karankawa and other coastal

tribes used baskets and the patterns they wove into their basketry.

Oil is found in much of the United States. It comes in various grades depending on several things, one of which is the base, or primary ingredient, of the oil. The highest-grade crude oil is purely paraffin based, while the lowest grade is purely asphalt based. Paraffin-based oil is found primarily in the East and for that reason is called "Pennsylvania-grade crude," since it was first found in Pennsylvania. As you move from east to west, asphalt gradually begins to replace paraffin as the base for the oil, and West Coast oil—"California-grade crude"—is totally asphalt based and the lowest grade of all. The celebrated La Brea Tar Pits near Los Angeles are simply ancient, very large oil springs from which all the volatile elements evaporated long ago, leaving only the sticky asphalt tar. Texas-grade crude oil is approximately half-paraffin and half-asphalt in base.

The first known use of Texas oil by Europeans occurred near Sabine Pass, Texas, in July of 1543. Several Spanish vessels—survivors of the DeSoto expedition headed home to Mexico—put into the mouth of a creek to seek shelter from a storm. On the surface of the water they found a dark, oily scum which they called copé. Since this copé looked and felt much like the pitch they used to caulk and seal their ships at home, and since—after being battered somewhat by the storm—the ships needed some caulking and sealing, they used it as they did pitch. There were, for years, numerous small underwater oil seeps near there, and as late as the mid-1940s this same dark, oily stuff could be found on the surface of creeks in that area from time to time.

The Indians, of course, knew about the oil seeps or oil springs in Texas and often bathed in them, used the oil as a medicinal salve, or even drank the stuff as medicine. According to Indian traditions, the early Spanish and French explorers visited some of their "medicine springs." Early Anglo settlers found oil springs in what are now Sabine, Shelby, Nacogdoches, San Augustine, Anderson, Grimes, Travis, Bexar, and Guadalupe counties, among others.

The earliest attempt to drill an oil well in Texas that we know of was in 1859 in Angelina County. A man named Jack Graham was hand-digging a water well when heavy crude oil seeped into the pit long before he struck water. Graham and several associates attempted to drill deeper, using a spring-pole drilling rig, but found little oil.

The family of Lynis T. Barrett moved to Melrose, Texas, from Virginia in 1832, bringing young Lynis along with them. There was a natural oil spring near Melrose, and Lynis, in later years, decided this curiosity of his youth had to be fed by an underground reservoir of oil. The commercial possibilities of petroleum as a base for lighting, heating fuel, and medicine had first been publicized by a Pennsylvanian as early as 1846. In 1860 Lynis T. Barrett arranged Texas' first oil lease for land belonging to the Skillern family, upon which the oil spring arose, for the purpose of drilling a well to provide oil. Before he could begin drilling, Texas seceded, and for the next four years Lynis was occupied by a grey coat and a musket.

On October 9, 1865, after Lee's surrender, Barrett renewed his lease on the oil spring. He brought in a peculiar rotary drilling machine. The bit was an eight-inch auger eight feet long, clamped to the bottom of a pipe. A cogwheel was attached to the top of the pipe, and the auger was turned by a drive shaft off a steam engine. The "drilling derrick" was a tripod made of wooden poles.

On September 12, 1866, while drilling at 100 feet, the auger suddenly dropped about six inches. The bit was pulled up, and the dirt sticking to the auger was found to be saturated with oil. About ten minutes later a small column of oil about four inches high bubbled up, making Barrett's first Texas oil well also the first—but nonspectacular—Texas gusher. Unfortunately for Barrett, oil prices were very low, the nearest refineries were in Pennsylvania, and as the political situation in Texas was "unsettled" due to reconstruction, he was unable to get anyone interested in his discovery. He and his Melrose Oil Company went broke.

Barrett may not have been the first. In 1847 Andrew Briscoe noted that from a shallow pond called Sour Lake, about 75 miles east of what is now central Houston, "sulphurous gas bubbles, and British oil or something very like it." There were several attempts to drill oil wells in the area, but none of them were reported as successful.

In 1868 Emory Starr and Peyton F. Edwards visited a place called Oil Spring in East Texas and dug into the sandy ground around the spring with spades. The next morning their holes were filled with water and oil. Some of the oil was taken to Nacogdoches, where it was used to oil harnesses.

Near Nacogdoches, up until the 1860s, there was an "oil mine." An underground deposit of a tarry substance had been located, and the tar-like stuff was mined with pick and shovel, brought to the surface, and literally squeezed under heavy pressure to force some oil out of it. The oil was mostly used as a lubricant.

It was in Nacogdoches, in 1887, that the Texas
oil industry really began. B. F. Hitchcock and
E. H. Farrar organized the Petroleum Prospecting
Company, brought in some experienced drillers
from Pennsylvania along with the state's first
cable-tool rig, and at 70 feet hit oil. It blew in—
though nowhere near as spectacularly as the great
gushers of later days—and flowed between 250 and
300 barrels onto the ground before it stopped.
By 1889 the PPC had drilled forty wells in the
Nacogdoches area, up to 100 feet deep. The company had an office shack, a storage barn with four
250-barrel wooden tanks in it and four more tanks
not yet assembled, two 1000-barrel iron tanks, an
engine house with a stationary engine in it, 14.5
miles of 3-inch pipeline leading from the field to
the railroad, and a 2000-barrel iron shipping tank
on the rails. By 1890 there were five oil companies
operating at the Nacogdoches field, with about 90
wells in production, and Texas' first—though
primitive—oil refinery was in operation there.

In 1878 Martin Meinsinger, who owned a
wagon yard in Brownwood, was hand-digging a
water well when, at a depth of 102 feet, he hit
oil-bearing sand which seeped about 5 gallons of
dark green oil per day. Meinsinger sold the oil as
lubricant and medicine—half a dollar a gallon as
lubricant, two bits per four-ounce bottle as medicine. In 1892 Meinsinger's well was still producing
and he was still selling the oil.

In 1886 George Dullnig, who owned a ranch six
miles southeast of the then city limits of San
Antonio, drilled for water but at 235 feet hit red-
dish-brown oil. He sold the stuff for from 20 to 35
cents per gallon depending on how much you
wanted. Fifteen feet from the first well he drilled
another, and at 300 feet he again hit oil. He then
drilled a third well, to 900 feet, but found no oil

below the 300-foot mark. Other pre-1900 wells were later drilled on the Dashiell farm near San Antonio, on the F. T. Walsh ranch near Sutherland Springs in Wilson County, and near Dunlay in Medina County.

Texas, in the 19th century, was also producing natural gas. R. G. Graham, in Young County, struck gas while drilling a water well in 1871. At the same time gas wells were found in Palo Pinto County, but they were regarded primarily as natural curiosities by locals. In 1879 through 1889 numerous gas wells were struck in Washington County, and the gas was used locally for heating and lighting. By 1889 the federal government listed Texas as an oil and gas producing state, recording that in that year Texas produced 48 barrels of oil and natural gas worth $1,728.

Long before 1901, Texas oil drillers were using many of the techniques that later came to characterize the great oil boom. In the 1890s the Baker brothers of Yankton, South Dakota, working in a shallow field near Corsicana, were the first to force water into the drill stem via a pump connected to a windmill, both lubricating the drill bit and washing the mud out of the casing to allow the oil to flow freely. A man named Chapman, working in the Nacogdoches area in the '80s, developed the flat rotary drilling table and used a home-built water-jet cable tool rig.

Yet all of this might not have happened, or at least not quite like it did, had not someone made Captain Richard King very mad.

When Texas became a state of the United States in February of 1846, it brought with it a heritage of Spanish/Mexican law. One of those laws regarded mineral rights, and it was a simple one—everything belonged to the king. The king of Spain—and later, by inheritance, the Republic of

Mexico, and by further inheritance, the Republic and State of Texas—held legal title to all surface and subsurface minerals of whatever type to be found within the boundaries of the state. Just incidentally, that law also applied to all game animals—they, too, were considered to belong to the king, but nobody ever pushed that one.

The law said, in effect, that a landowner owned the surface of the ground and that which grew on it, those animals which he put on it and their increase, and the rights to water to irrigate the farmland and water his stock, but nothing else. If any minerals—and, of course, by "minerals" the Spanish always meant precious metals or stones— were found upon or in the land, they belonged to the king (and later to Mexico or Texas) and the king had the sole right to award mining concessions for them to whomever he pleased, with or without the landowner's consent.

Texans didn't really pay a lot of attention to this law until 1866. There was, upon the vast expanse of land to which Captain Richard King and his partner, Mifflin Kenedy, obtained title, a huge deposit of surface salt called El Sal Del Rey— "The King's Salt." It had been there for millennia, and the animals and Indians had certainly never asked permission to take salt for their own use from it. Neither did Richard King. It was on his land, and he assumed—quite naturally—that it was his salt. He didn't begrudge anyone salt—there was a seemingly unlimited supply—and his neighbors came from miles around to gather salt for their own use at El Sal Del Rey.

In 1866 a martial-law state government was installed in Austin, controlled by the Union army and under the thumb of such virulent anti-Southerners as Thaddeus Stevens and Charles Sumner of Massachusetts. Stephens and Sumner, in particular, were determined to destroy the South's economy—including that of Texas—so thoroughly that the former Confederacy could never again be anything but a group of "conquered provinces." Various unpleasant people—called "carpetbaggers" for their alleged practice of carrying all their worldly goods in a small valise made of carpet so they could scoot quickly if necessary—came south to participate in the destruction and looting of whatever the war had left of the Southern economy.

A group of these carpetbaggers went to Austin and got—quite legally, and in accordance with then-existing state law—the exclusive state concession to gather and sell salt from El Sal Del Rey. They established an office in Corpus Christi and set up a salt-gathering operation on King's ranch.

Richard King decided his ranch needed salt, so he sent several men with a wagon to get some from the salt flat. They were met by rifle-armed carpetbaggers, who informed them that their company now owned, by state concession, the sole right to gather salt from El Sal Del Rey, and if Captain King wanted salt, he'd have to go to Corpus Christi and buy it just like everybody else.

Richard King must have been having an off-day, because he didn't personally go out and turn the whole crew into shark bait. Instead, he went to Austin—and he was mad!

King went to the Texas Supreme Court and put his case before it. In what is called, to this day, The Sal Del Rey Decision, the Texas Supreme Court ruled that the entire body of Texas mineral law was "contrary to Anglo-Saxon tradition and usage" (it wasn't—all European monarchies, including the English monarchy, were considered to "own" all minerals and game in the realm). The law was therefore void *ab initio*—from the beginning. The state concession to dig salt on the King ranch was invalid because the law that allowed it was not just void, but had never been legal to begin with.

That decision—rendered because Captain Richard King got mad when a bunch of dam-Yankees wouldn't let him dig salt on his own land —laid the foundation for Texas' great oil industry and for every oil fortune ever made or ever to be made in Texas. By voiding the Spanish/Mexican law, U.S. law came into play, and in the United States a landowner, unless he had otherwise disposed of them, owned the rights to all minerals on and under his land and the rights to all game that ran on it. Every oil operator in Texas should, by rights, keep a portrait of Richard King and a small container of salt in a shrine in his office—but I'll bet not a one does.

If there is one word in the English language that will evoke the great days of Texas' oil industry, that one word is *SPINDLETOP!* It is a word that should forever be printed in italics and capitalized, for at approximately 10:00 A.M. on January 10, 1901, atop what was known as Sour Spring Hill, near Beaumont, Texas, not far from a peculiar tree named "Spindletop" for its inverted-cone shape, the whole world changed. The Oil Age literally "blew in."

It wasn't that no one knew there was oil around Sour Spring Hill—it was oil that gave the water from the springs in and around the hill its sour taste. Desultory drilling had gone on around it for several years, but no one had hit anything significant. All previous wells had stopped no deeper than 450 feet, where they hit a treacherous formation of shifting "quicksands" called The Gumbo. Either the available drilling technology, the patience of the backers, or the money ran out before anyone was able to devise a way to drill through The Gumbo and hit the oil that was surely there.

On June 20, 1899, the Gladys City Oil, Gas, and Manufacturing Company, which owned drilling rights to Sour Spring Hill, gave a lease to Captain A. F. Lucas of Washington, D.C.—an Austrian-born mining engineer with a lot of salt-dome experience behind him in Louisiana. Lucas drilled a 575-foot test well and actually bailed out a little oil, but his personal money ran out and he couldn't find local backers to continue the drilling. He went to Guffey and Galey, a Pennsylvania operation that had worked extensively near Corsicana. Guffey and Galey—later Gulf Oil Corporation—assumed control of the Gladys City company and secured a 20-year lease on Sour Spring Hill on September 18, 1900.

In the fall of 1900 Beaumont, the closest town to Sour Spring Hill, was a small, sleepy Gulf Coast town with little major commercial activity. The best farmland around could be bought for $40 per acre, while the land around Sour Spring Hill, which wasn't fertile because of the seeping oil, sold for as little as $10 per acre. There were about 10,000 people in the town, and the only two banks—First National and Beaumont National—could boast combined deposits of but $661,818. The major industries were logging in the pine forests around town and some shallow-draft shipping on the Neches River.

Captain Lucas hired the Hamill brothers, who'd worked for Guffey and Galey in Corsicana, to drill his new test well at Sour Spring Hill. Al Hamill was the driller, his brother Curt was what we would call, today, the tool pusher, and Henry McLeod and Peck Byrd were the rest of the drilling crew. Byrd, the fireman on the steam-powered rig, had to contend with water-soaked firewood bought from the Beaumont Lumber Company's local mill, and he had a difficult time keeping a head of steam that would run the engine to turn the drill.

At 160 feet the well lost water circulation—water was used to lubricate the bit—and from there until 445 feet, when the well reached The Gumbo, Al had to use the cathead as a pile-driving rig, literally pounding the hole into the ground rather than drilling it. In the shifting sands of The Gumbo, the water used to lubricate the drillbit in the hole disappeared into the sand. Curt Hamill reasoned that if the water were muddy—or a thin, flowable mud were used—the lubrication might not be lost. He made a watertank by building a dam around about an acre and a half of clayey soil, pumped it full of water, and hired a neighbor to drive his cows up and down the tank until the water was churned into thin mud. The mud didn't disappear in the hole. Today the making and selling of specially formulated, chemically laden "mud" as a drilling lubricant is a major part of the oil industry.

Two hundred feet further down, the circulating mud began to boil up and flow through the table, and shortly afterwards a column of muddy water and gas spewed from the hole halfway up the 70-foot wooden derrick. It subsided quickly, and the drillers decided they had hit a gas pocket. The blowout had filled the slush pit with sand, which had to be shoveled out by hand.

McLeod, deciding that the work was too hard and the return too little, quit, requiring the remaining three-man crew to go on 18-hour shifts. All three men would work a regular 12-hour shift through the day, then alternate to one man working an 18-hour shift every third day, in order to keep the drilling going all night. It was necessary to keep the bit turning slowly all the time to prevent a gas blowout and to prevent the drill pipe from sticking.

On the night of December 9, 1900, it was Al Hamill's turn to pull the 18 hours. He recorded that he was "trying to make all the hole I could." A new length of drill pipe had been attached, and apparently not much hole had been made during the day, for most of it was still above the table. At about 3 A.M. Al noticed that the pump began to work more freely, and very shortly the entire new section of pipe had disappeared into the hole. With dawn the drillers noticed a showing of oil in the slush pit, and Captain Lucas was sent for. He asked Al how much of a well he thought they'd make, and Al said it certainly ought to make 50 barrels a day.

Another section of pipe was put on and the well gained about another 35 feet of easy going, then hit a hard formation at 880 feet. Soft sand had entered the pipe and come up about 300 feet, and it was saturated with oil. The well was washed, and drilling continued.

On December 24 the drilling shut down for Christmas, then resumed on January 1. By January 7 the hole was down to 1020 feet, at which point it seemed to hit a crevice in the subsurface rock, driving the bit off-center. On January 9 Al telegraphed Corsicana to get a fishtail bit, which he hoped would put the hole back on track. It arrived by rail that night, and the following morning the pipe was pulled, the new bit attached, and the process of lowering the drill pipe back into the hole began.

When 700 feet of pipe had been lowered into the hole, the drilling mud once again began forcing up through the table. It suddenly increased in power, spewing mud halfway up the derrick and

drenching Curt Hamill, who was on the double
boards. He came down quickly. Just as he hit the
ground the drill pipe itself shot upwards out of the
hole, knocking the crown block off the derrick and
breaking apart as it rose. A blast of gas followed,
and then the well was quiet.

Deciding that the show was over and it was
time to clean up the mess it made, the crew
grabbed shovels and headed back for the drill
floor. About the time they began shoveling there
was a terrific blast, a huge column of heavy mud
shot upwards, and then from deep in the ground
came a loud, continuing roar. This was followed
by gas, then several short but powerful spurts of
oil—oilmen call them "head flows"—which increased in size and volume. These were followed
by a volley of rocks that shot several hundred feet
in the air. Then, at just about 10 A.M., it happened.
A powerful, continuous stream of oil, increasing
in speed and volume, shot upward 150 feet like a
fountain, then rained down on the countryside
around Sour Spring Hill. Lucas #1—SPINDLETOP
—had blown in! Texas' oil age had arrived.

Until the Lucas gusher, Texas had measured its
annual oil production by the hundreds of 42–
gallon barrels the state produced per year. Lucas
#1 blew out an estimated 75,000 barrels of oil
every 24 hours it gushed—nearly half as much oil,
during the time it flowed, as all other Texas fields
combined had produced since the first successful
well was drilled, and more oil in five days than the
total yearly production of all the oilfields in
Pennsylvania—and it took nine days to cap it off! It
was the first true gusher—the first of many Texas
was to produce as the tremendous underground
reservoir of oil upon which much of the state
rested was tapped.

In order to cap the well and stop the waste of oil—roughly 42,000,000 gallons of it in those nine days—the Hamill brothers constructed a sort of rail line of wood running on each side of the column of oil. A small rail-car-like structure was built on the "rails"—but secured so that instead of simply rolling on them, it couldn't be easily jerked off them upwards. Inside the "rail car" there was an 8" diameter pipe nipple topped by a large Tee, which had 8" gate valves attached to the top and side. The "rail car" was forced into and over the spouting column of oil until the oil spouted out the top of the Tee, through the top valve. The nipple was then collared and bolted to the well casing, and the top valve was closed. With the powerful flow of oil now going out the side rather than the top of the well, the base of the valve assembly was caulked with oakum and tightly secured to the well casing. Finally the second valve was closed, and Lucas #1—the first gusher—was under control. The hardware has been improved, but essentially the same system is used to control a "wild well" today.

In country where land had recently sold for $10 per acre, 25x34 foot blocks—just large enough for a derrick and engine—now sold for $6000. Farmland that had been selling for $40 per acre was now cut into 1/5 acre lots and sold for as high as $40,000 per lot. Land up to 150 miles from Beaumont was bringing as high as $1000 per acre, and one acre within the proven field sold for $900,000. Derricks were built so close together that plank runways were built from derrick to derrick at the upper levels so crewmen could escape in case of fire.

By the middle of July 1901, Beaumont's population had increased from 10,000 to 30,000, and the town's four banks—two more were opened—

boasted combined deposits of $3,369,587.40. Oil
was so plentiful it sold at the wellhead for three
cents per 42-gallon barrel—while an eight-ounce
cup of clean, relatively cool drinking water cost a
nickel, and it required fifty barrels of oil to raise
the dollar and a half a bottle of beer went for.

Oilfield geology, during the early days of the oil
industry, has been described as "part guesswork,
part witchcraft, and mostly dumb luck," and the
description is accurate. In East Texas, oil fields had
been found where there were surface indications
of oil, but what happened where there weren't any
surface indications? Well, you went at it by guess
and by gosh, and if you were right you got rich,
and if you weren't you either got broke real fast or
kept trying until you either went dead broke or hit
oil. "Truisms" were exploded daily—like the one
that said "there isn't any oil in the Panhandle."
Some of Texas' biggest oilfields—though they were
deep-well fields—were found in the Panhandle.
Then there was "there isn't any oil west of the
Pecos." Iraan and a half-dozen other West Texas
boom towns came from oil that "wasn't," west of
the Pecos.

Iraan—which is pronounced Ira-ann, by the
way, not "iran," and was named for Ira and Ann,
the original owners of the ranch on which it was
built—gave us something besides oil. Victor T.
Hamlin, a young draftsman working as a map-
maker for an oil company in the oil camp that later
became Iraan, watched bulldozers and scrapers,
preparing the ground for the erection of drilling
rigs, scrape up dinosaur bones by the truckload.
It gave him an idea, and the idea became the
well-known V. T. Hamlin comic strip, "Alley Oop."
Iraan's public park, today, is called "Alley Oop
Fantasy Land" and features characters from
Hamlin's cartoons.

For a long time it seemed that there was no place in Texas you couldn't find oil. Texas has 254 counties, ranging in size from tiny Rockwall County, barely five miles on a side, to Brewster County, which is the largest subprovincial political subdivision in the world, larger than several New England states and some European countries. (We used to have 255 counties until Oklahoma stole one, but that's another story.) Oil has been found in 214 of the 254 counties Texas still has. One of the forty unfortunates that has never produced so much as a single drop of petroleum, most folks are surprised to learn, is Dallas County. Oil is found to within 30 miles of the Dallas County line, but none has ever been located in Dallas County.

The little town of Kilgore, deep in the piney woods of East Texas on the Harrison/Rusk County line, boasted more oil wells than people. At the height of the East Texas oil boom, Kilgore had about 17,000 people—and more than 30,000 producing wells in the city limits alone. Oil wells—with accompanying wooden and later steel derricks—sprouted from front yards, back yards, in public parks, and on the school ground. As one old Kilgore native put it, "We didn't have monkey bars on the school ground—didn't need 'em. We had an oil derrick to climb on." One well was literally in the middle of a downtown department store—the well operated inside a walled-off section of the building while shoppers bought goods all around it and the derrick stuck through an opening in the roof.

Old-time oilmen can remember when "the sun never set in Kilgore." The natural gas that accompanied much Texas oil was laden with hydrogen sulfide, and for years the technology to remove its overwhelmingly foul rotten-egg odor did not exist.

Oilmen simply piped the stinking, sulfur-laden gas up a tall standpipe and set fire to it—called "flaring it off" in oilfield terminology. Kilgore, though its gas was "sweet"—that is, not sulfur-laden—simply had too much gas and no way to get rid of it. For years the town was brightly lit by day with the hot Texas sun and by night with gas flares, and Kilgore children literally had to leave town to visit relatives to see what "night" actually looked like. For over ten years you couldn't see the stars from anywhere inside Kilgore's city limits—the night was too brightly lit with gas flares. Blackout restrictions during WW II finally extinguished Kilgore's perpetual daylight. After World War II ended, technological developments that made it possible to filter the hydrogen sulfide out of the natural gas and allow it to be used for heating and an increased demand for natural gas across the nation finally shut down nearly all the gas flares in Texas.

A note here—pure methane or "natural gas" is absolutely odorless. The "gas" you smell when the pilot light in the stove goes out is not the smell of the gas itself, but of a chemical added to it to give it a distinctive odor. That odor is there because of something that happened in New London, Texas, in 1937.

New London, in the East Texas oil patch, was making use of locally available natural gas—almost pure, and therefore virtually odorless—to heat its public buildings, among them the community school. A gas leak developed, saturating the school with highly explosive natural gas. The resulting explosion killed over 300 people—most of them elementary school children—and resulted in legislation requiring an additive to natural gas to make it stink so you could tell when the gas was leaking.

Considering the amount of money to be made from oil and the amount of drilling that was going on, you would suspect that somewhere along the line it would be necessary to regulate the industry. The earliest regulations were set by the major oil companies, mostly requiring the spacing of derricks and cleanup around them to prevent oilfield fires. The most stringent regulations were actually set by Dan Waggoner, owner of the 600,000-acre Sacahuista Ranch near Vernon, Texas.

Dan Waggoner was a cattleman. When a water well, being drilled on his ranch, brought up oil—good oil, and apparently lots of it—he ordered the well capped off and the drilling rig moved to a new spot. "My cows can't drink oil," he said.

Oil drilling eventually moved into the area around Waggoner's Sacahuista Ranch, and finally old Dan permitted drilling—on his terms. Waggoner, not the oil companies, specified how far apart the wells had to be. Waggoner specified when and where drilling could take place and what precautions were to be taken to prevent spilling oil on the ground or in cleaning up spills. There is a story—probably as true as any other—that tells of an oil company scout who got lost for three days on Waggoner's vast ranch. When he was found he was asked if he was hungry. "Of course not," he snorted. "There are enough 'provisions' in a Waggoner lease to keep a man going for six months."

Unfortunately, not all landowners were as careful about what went on when drilling started as was Dan Waggoner. East Texas fields in particular wasted a lot of oil, but Texas oilmen, at least, did their best to cap "wild wells"—gushers. In Arkansas, in the Smackover Oil Field, wild wells were allowed to flow until they stopped on their own. Millions, possibly billions, of barrels of oil were foolishly wasted, several thousand square miles of pine and hardwood forest that once stood over the Smackover field were destroyed, and to this day the land will not produce anything but oil, and—nowadays—not much of that.

With all the oil drilling and production, the price of oil fell steadily. Even with the rise in popularity of the automobile, there was simply too much oil being produced. With the coming of the Great Depression in 1929, trouble came to the oil fields. Production was high, but the price of oil fell so low that even heavily producing fields were operating at a loss. Something had to be done.

Texas governor Ross S. Sterling (1931-1933) asked the Texas Railroad Commission—the only regulatory body in Texas government at the time— to take control of the oil fields and limit production in order to raise oil prices. Major oil companies went along happily, but the independents—small producers who saw an attempt at regulation to be a threat to their meager incomes— resisted. The Railroad Commission set "allowable" —the maximum amount of oil that could be produced in the state in a month—and prorated the "allowable" over the producing companies on the basis of the number of wells a company had in production. Obviously, if a company was a big one, with a thousand wells in production, it did well, but if it was a small company, with only one or two wells producing, the "allowable" reduced its already-small profit.

The result was "hot oil"—oil produced over the allowable, which was transported and sold on an illegal black market. The "hot oil" reduced the overall price of oil by competing with the wells that were producing under the "allowable" system and putting more oil into the game than the price could support. Refineries, mostly out of state but some within the state, were perfectly willing to buy "hot oil" at below-market prices and process it, since once it entered a storage tank no one could tell if it was "hot"—illegally produced—or not.

In order to stop the flow of "hot oil" from Texas oil fields—mostly East Texas fields—Governor Sterling called out the Texas Rangers, mobilized the Texas National Guard, and declared martial law in the oil fields. (The Rangers, at that time, were both part of the Texas State Militia system under the adjutant general and the only statewide police force Texas had.) Between the Rangers and the National Guard the "hot oil" business, while not shut down completely, was reduced to a level that the sale of "hot oil" didn't noticeably reduce the price of legally produced oil. The move proved very unpopular in East Texas, though, where many local people felt that the governor had done them wrong by limiting the amount of oil that could be taken from their property and therefore the amount of money they, as landowners, would receive in royalty payments from oil companies. Ross Sterling served only one term as governor and was defeated in his bid for reelection, but today he is recognized as the man who saved the oil business in Texas during the Depression.

SOURCES

Many of these stories—and much of the detail that goes into the telling of others—are derived from what J. Frank Dobie, in *Coronado's Children*, called "The Grasshopper's Library." This marvelous library, seldom used these days, consists of tales told and retold around campfires, across cafe tables or bars, or over crockery cups filled with coffee boiled in blue-granite pots in the kitchens of farm houses or ranch houses. The Grasshopper's Library is no less than the oral heritage of the people of Texas—an oral heritage that is being rapidly lost, to be replaced by thirty-minute television advertisements in which small, mindless creatures beat one another over the head with nameless objects of strange shape in order to sell plastic replicas of the creatures and objects to children at outrageous prices.

The Grasshopper's Library encompasses, but is not limited to, the collected archives of the Shadetree Historical Society, whose members may not always tell history as it was, but certainly tell it as it oughta been.

Beyond The Grasshopper's Library there is another library, and it sits on shelves in my office or on shelves at the public library building in almost any town—or, unfortunately, in ever-decreasing amounts, on shelves in bookstores. Texans have a love affair with the history of Texas, and rightly so. They tend to write books about that history—and they tend to buy those books and occasionally actually read them. The books have ranged, over the years, from meticulously researched history to wild speculation; from the scrupulously accurate to the out-and-out lie. They all have their place, and it is up to the reader to discern which is which. A word to the wise, though—I've found that the lies generally aren't nearly as much fun as the truth.

The following books, among others, furnished material for this book—either the genesis and factual background for the stories, or the way to check a story already heard. All are well worth reading.

Almaraz, Felix D, Jr. *Tragic Cavalier, Governor Manuel Salcedo of Texas, 1808-1813.* Austin: University of Texas Press, 1971.

Brice, Donaly E. *The Great Comanche Raid.* Austin: Eakin Press, 1987.

Cutrer, Thomas W., Ph. D. *The English Texans.* San Antonio: University of Texas Institute of Texan Cultures, 1985.

Davis, John L., Ph. D. *Exploration in Texas, Ancient and Otherwise, With Thoughts on the Nature of Evidence.* San Antonio: University of Texas Institute of Texan Cultures, 1984.

Dobie, J. Frank. *Coronado's Children.* Garden City, New York: Garden City Publishing Co., 1930.

Duval, John C. *Early Times in Texas, or The Adventures of Jack Dobell.* Lincoln, Nebraska: University of Nebraska Press, Bison Books reprint, 1986.

Eckhardt, C. F. *The Lost San Saba Mines.* Austin: Texas Monthly Press, 1981.

Garrett, Julia Kathryn, Ph. D. *Green Flag Over Texas.* New York and Dallas: Cordova Press, 1939.

Hogan, William Ransom. *The Texas Republic, A Social and Economic History.* Norman, Oklahoma: University of Oklahoma Press, 1946.

Pickrell, Annie Doom. *Pioneer Women In Texas.* Austin: privately printed, (no date).

Rister, Carl Coke. *Oil! Titan of the Southwest.* Norman, Oklahoma: University of Oklahoma Press, 1949.

Schwarz, Ted, and Thonhoff, Robert H. *Forgotten Battlefield of the First Texas Revolution: The Battle of Medina, August 18, 1813.* Austin: Eakin Press, 1985.

Siegel, Stanley. *A Political History of the Texas Republic, 1836-1845.* Austin: University of Texas Press, 1956.

Smithwick, Noah. *Evolution of a State.* Austin: University of Texas Press, 1982 (reprint).

Syers, William Edward. *Ghost Stories of Texas.* Waco: Texian Press, 1981.

Wilbarger, J. W. *Indian Depredations In Texas.* Austin: Hutchings Printing House, 1889.

Williams, J. W. *Old Texas Trails.* Burnet: Eakin Press, 1979.

And

The Grasshoppers' Library, courtesy The Shadetree Historical Society

Index